HEAR THE BEAT

HEAR THE BEAT

Elizabeth Neill

The Book Guild Ltd
Sussex, England

First published in Great Britain in 2002 by
The Book Guild Ltd
25 High Street,
Lewes, East Sussex
BN7 2LU

Copyright © Elizabeth Neill 2002

The right of Elizabeth Neill to be identified as the author of this work has been asserted by her in accordance with the Copyright, Designs and Patents Act 1988.

All rights reserved. No part of this publication may be reproduced, transmitted, or stored in a retrieval system, in any form or by any means, without permission in writing from the publisher, nor be otherwise circulated in any form of binding or cover other than that in which it is published and without a similar condition being imposed on the subsequent purchaser.

All characters in this publication are fictitious and any resemblance to real people, alive or dead, is purely coincidental.

Typesetting in Baskerville by
Keyboard Services, Luton, Bedfordshire

Printed in Great Britain by
Bookcraft (Bath) Ltd, Avon

A catalogue record for this book is available from
The British Library.

ISBN 1 85776 621 0

I would like to dedicate my book *Hear The Beat* to three special people.

Paul Sugg, my fitness trainer, who got me 'moving' again after the trauma of major surgery and who inspired me to write this book. My thanks to you, Paul.

Gary Baitz, our vet, who fought so hard to save our Labrador, Holly's life. Thank you for all your kindness to us then and now, Gary.

Ken Mears, who has helped me all along the way to produce my manuscript, just as he did when I wrote my family saga. Many thanks, once again, Ken.

1

The pub on Wimbledon Common where Tom and David had just shared a bar snack and a bottle of wine was filled to capacity. They had been very fortunate to secure the last table in the dining area, and it was near an open log fire which had proved very congenial for them.

David looked at Tom and said, 'Your news is incredibly hard for me to take on board. First your dog is diagnosed with a heart condition and after the finest attention dies, and now, less than two months on, you're telling me that you also have a heart condition and are going into the world's leading hospital to have major heart surgery!'

'I'm afraid it's all true!' exclaimed Tom. 'It might be the biggest coincidence, but I can assure you, that's the way it is. All I can say at this point is that I hope my heart problems will prove to have a happier outcome than my poor Holly's did.'

Tom remembered, only too painfully, the fight they had put up for Holly's life. She was a beautiful, eight-year-old, yellow Labrador, who had never had a day's illness in her life. She had started to present problems just prior to Christmas, like backing away from her food, which was so unlike her. Labradors have a reputation for loving their food and they would gladly eat all day long, given the chance. Tom had spent most of the Christmas period coping with his very sick dog, including spending all Boxing Day morning at the vet's surgery. The vet had carried out numerous tests on Holly and given her injections, he had changed her diet and warned Tom that her heart beat was very erratic. The whole of Christmas had been a time of concern for Holly's rapid deterioration.

The vet, Gary, had done everything in his power to save her, but four days after Christmas he had to admit defeat. He told Tom that the only chance for Holly was to take her up to Cambridge University's Department of Clinical Veterinary Medicine. If there was a place where they could save her life – it would be there in Cambridge. They had wanted to give her a pacemaker, as Holly's lower heart now presented a third-degree blockage. But it never happened, as after a week spent in the Veterinary Hospital, Holly's heart gave up entirely and she literally stopped breathing.

It was one of the saddest scenarios Tom could remember and he was still haunted by guilt as well as sadness. The guilt he felt was for the fact that he had not been with his beloved dog when she died and he wondered, many a time, whether she had not only felt desperately ill at the end, but also that she had been abandoned in her final days. Tom would never know. All he did know was that he wished he had never taken her up to Cambridge, although it had been the only chance of saving her life.

The shock which Tom was experiencing now was bringing Holly very much to the fore. It was almost as if Holly had heralded what was about to happen in his own life and it was a frightening feeling.

David broke the silence between the two friends. 'I always thought that you were the fittest man in the world, Tom! You certainly always give me the impression that you are. How on earth could a thing like this happen to you, of all people? For heaven's sake, you're a personal fitness trainer, an aerobics teacher, a ski instructor, a yoga teacher – so what's gone wrong?'

'Mind-blowing stuff, isn't it?' replied Tom with a warm smile which masked his fear. 'If you wonder what's gone wrong, just imagine what thoughts are racing through my mind! My mother and my father both died of heart attacks in their early sixties, and neither of them was into the fitness scene. They both smoked and probably didn't exercise enough, so I expect a lot of my problems could be genetic ones.'

'Well, I suppose that could be part of it,' replied David. 'But your lifestyle is so healthy. If you're not teaching fitness, you're riding, skiing, walking, jogging, climbing mountains, dancing – you name it, you're doing it. Action man, eat your heart out! Sorry, Tom, wrong choice of words.'

'I probably have put a lot of strain on the old ticker, if the truth be known. But to me there have never been enough hours in the day to do all that I want to do and I always live in the fast lane.'

Tom drove his car home and had to admit to himself that it was a relief to get his problems off his chest to David. Their friendship had spanned many years and they had shared quite a few adventures along life's journey. Tom could imagine how devastated David would have been with his particular news and knew that he would dwell on the enormity of it all.

Tom switched the engine of his car off in his driveway and got out and walked over to his front door. Before turning the key in the latch, he looked down at the doorstep and remembered how six weeks ago a neat parcel had been sitting there. He had picked it up and taken it into the kitchen, where he had carefully opened the Jiffy bag. Inside, Tom had discovered a brown, wooden, carved box, which contained Holly's ashes. If it hadn't been so sad, it would have been macabre. Your dog sent to you through the post. Yes, Holly did come home, but certainly not in the way that Tom had intended.

2

Tom lay on his back perfectly still with his eyes closed. Everywhere was in total silence, apart from the occasional baying of the fox – its deep prolonged tones sounded somewhat creepy in the early hours. Tom guessed that it was somewhere around two in the morning, but felt too comfortable to reach over to turn his bedside lamp on to look at his clock.

Thoughts were racing around in his mind: his forthcoming operation, sorting out his business, delegating his clients to another fitness trainer, his home, his cats, in fact, everything and anything that he was involved with. Also, he had to cancel a ski holiday that was scheduled in two weeks' time, when he would have been half teaching and half holidaying. It was now the month of March and Tom was due to do a sponsored walk in June on the Great Wall of China in order to help underprivileged children. The sponsors had been coming in thick and fast, but he would have to postpone the walk for a future date. Everything in life would be coming to a standstill, whilst Tom's surgeon exercised his skills, prior to a three-month recovery and convalescent period. Tom needed to put his house in order and this was proving to be quite a major task in itself.

Tom knew that he must tell Nicola what was about to happen to him. He realized that he had told everyone else except Nicola and he wondered how she would react to his news. His thoughts went back to the one and only night that he had ever spent with her. It had been the most precious and memorable night of his entire life and he was just thankful that he had had that time with her. Nicola was, beyond any doubt his ideal woman – she was everything that he had ever desired. But she was married to his friend, Graham Ross, and so that, in Tom's reckoning, ruled her out for himself. Graham certainly didn't deserve to have Nicola as his wife. Graham had played around ever since his marriage and, despite their twins, Andrew and Sophie, he behaved as a bachelor with a real roving eye. Tom thought what a fool he was to keep on putting his marriage and his children at risk.

Poor Nicola, she had plenty to contend with, but she still managed to battle on. To her, the family came first and she had turned a blind eye on more than one occasion to Graham's indiscretions. Tom liked to think that he had become Nicola's number one confidant over the years and her shoulder to cry on, although Tom felt far more for Nicola than friendship. Tom loved her with every fibre of his body and soul, but apart from that one night in the French Alps, he had kept his feelings locked away and well under control.

What a wonderful night that had been! Tom had been on a skiing holiday with Nicola and Graham but Graham had not wanted to go up on the high slopes, so Tom and Nicola had gone up alone. Then a sudden storm had cut them off before they could ski down the mountain and they had been forced to spend the night together in a refuge hut. They had been safe inside and had expressed their love for one another both verbally and physically. Tom had promised Nicola the following morning that their secret night of passion would go with him to his grave. Tom also told Nicola that he would always be there for her, either as her lover, her husband, her confidant, her friend. In other words, Tom would be whatever she wanted him to be to her. She had chosen his friendship.

It was about five years since the incident and yet it only felt like yesterday in Tom's mind, so vivid was his recollection. That night their passion for one another had known no bounds, but Nicola's loyalty lay with her husband, and her duty and love belonged to her children. Despite the passing years, time did nothing to diminish Tom's desire for Nicola, and in his heart of hearts, he knew that the feeling was reciprocal.

Since that night, Tom had respected Nicola's choice and had kept his distance. He loved and admired her from afar, but, nevertheless, he was always there for her. Their times spend alone were pretty well non-existent, but now with his forthcoming operation just over a week away and the risk that it involved, Tom was determined to telephone her to arrange a meeting. He needed to talk to her and it was his turn to need that special shoulder to cry on.

Tom knew that it was because of his love for Nicola that he himself had chosen to remain a bachelor; no other woman had ever come up to his expectations and Nicola was a very hard act to follow. Despite the absence of a wife in his life, Tom had had his fair share of lady friends and was very popular with the opposite sex. He was forty-seven and still a very eligible man, but he wasn't looking for a wife.

Tom's over-active mind and tired body eventually gave in to sleep and he managed to get his well-earned rest for another hour or two.

3

'Where would you like me to take you for dinner?' asked Tom, forcing himself to sound as normal as possible, hoping that the actual anxiety he was feeling did not come across on the telephone.

'You say where, Tom,' replied Nicola. 'I'm more than a little intrigued why you need to see me so urgently! Has something happened? You're not getting married or leaving the country, are you?'

'No! Nothing like that. But I do need to see you, and the sooner the better.'

'Well, Graham is away at a managers' conference in Brighton for a couple of days, so I could get my mother to sit with the twins. Either this evening or tomorrow, it really depends which one suits you the best – I know you often see clients in the evening.'

'Let's leave it that you talk to your mother and then could you get back to me? Tonight or tomorrow are both fine with me,' said Tom, and was tempted to add that he was pleased that Graham was away, but decided not to make any comment. Most probably he would have ended up having dinner with both of them and that's the last thing he wanted. It was Nicola he needed to see and it was a bonus for him that Graham happened to be in Brighton.

'That's fine, Tom,' replied Nicola. 'You've got me really guessing about what your important news is – I can't wait! I'll phone you back as soon as I can get hold of my mother.'

Tom replaced the telephone receiver very slowly. Little did Nicola know what news he really had and he wasn't looking forward one little bit to having to tell her. He imagined her reaction would be the same as those of his friends and clients, in a single word, disbelief. He could understand their reaction; after all was said and done, he was the one who was supposed to be ultra fit! Tom spent his working days teaching his clients how to use their limbs and muscles correctly. He told them how to keep the heart fit and how to keep everything in good working order, even after major illnesses and operations. It was quite unbelievable that this was happening to him, of all people!

An hour later, Tom's telephone rang and he answered it in his study.

Nicola's familiar voice said, 'It's only me. Just to let you know that there is no problem for my mother to come to look after the terrible twins! She says tonight would be the most convenient for her and she'll stay overnight. That means, either we can go out to eat locally or we could go up to town, as time is no obstacle. The choice is yours.'

'That's great, Nicola! It'll be nice not to have a deadline to keep and it gives me a chance to spend a little time with you.' Tom nearly added that he would like to spend all his time with her, but restrained himself. 'I'll pick you up at seven thirty and take you somewhere really special for dinner!' Tom hadn't yet made up his mind at this stage where he was going to take her, but he would sort it out during the day.

He glanced at his watch. His first client had cancelled this morning, but he was due to see the next one in half an hour's time. This client lived in Roehampton, very near to the gates leading into Richmond Park.

It was gloriously sunny, bitterly cold but bright – just the sort of day that Tom liked. He could work outside with his client rather than indoors, which he was forced to do when the weather was against him. Tom would suggest a 'power' walk to his client, which was a walk intended to raise the heart beat and which produced a feeling of well being, both for Tom and his clients.

'The heart': everything revolved around the heart and yet, how natural it was to take its steady beat from cradle to grave for granted!

His client, Jane Shepherd, was a lady in her late fifties, who had undergone a very serious operation for bowel cancer about five years ago. Jane, through a member of her family, had asked Tom if he would be able to get her fit again. Tom had taken up the challenge without a moment's hesitation, but had first to approach Jane's doctor to see if it was all right to proceed with the training. Once he was given the green light, he had trained Jane twice a week and they had become firm friends.

Tom was very pleased with the results as Jane had virtually no movement in her abdomen to start with, due to all the cutting the surgeon had had to do through the muscles, but now, over the months, all the training had paid dividends. Jane had become increasingly mobile and flexible and had regained her confidence to cope with life. Tom had put Jane on a regime of exercise, yoga, walking and stretching, which she really enjoyed doing. Tom couldn't help wondering this morning how he would feel after his major surgery and if he would 'bounce back' as successfully as Jane had done. Only time would tell!

4

'You can't be serious!' said Nicola, putting her wine glass down and studying Tom's face as if she was seeing him for the first time this evening.

'I promise you, Nicky, it's all true,' replied Tom, imagining the shock he must have given her.

'Tom! I can't get my mind around what you've just said – you, of all people! You don't abuse your body in any way – quite the reverse, you look after it much more than the average person does. So what on earth's gone wrong?'

'Good question! I only wish that I knew the answer to it, but I'm obviously not as fit as I thought I was – my image is slipping!' said Tom, trying to make light of it. His time with Nicola was precious and he didn't want to become too morbid.

'Then how did you know that there was anything wrong with you in the first place?' asked Nicola kindly.

'Well, it all began with a tightness that I experienced in my chest at high levels of physical exertion. My doctor referred me to a cardiologist after I complained to him of a mild cramping in my chest. In turn, the cardiologist performed a "stress ECG", which monitors the heart under varying loads. At rest and at moderate load, my heart appeared perfectly normal, however, at a more intense level of exercise, my heart did show signs of distress. He recommended me to have an angiogram, which takes internal pictures of the heart, and it showed up a number of narrowings in the coronary arteries.' Tom stopped, wondering if he was becoming a little too technical.

'What happened next?' asked Nicola with a growing concern for Tom, whom she had always regarded as her rock to lean on in her times of trouble.

'I was then faced with three options: medication, angioplasty or surgery, and, after having discussed them all with my cardiologist, I've chosen to have surgery. With surgery, the blocked arteries are bypassed using arteries or veins obtained from another part of the body, and in my case they will be taken from my chest. The risk of recurrence is very small if I follow a sensible lifestyle after my operation, which I have every intention of doing.'

A silence followed as Nicola tried her hardest to absorb what Tom had just told her and it wasn't easy to take in, as Tom had always been so healthy and fit. Everyone else seemed to get things wrong with them, but never Tom!

Finally Nicola broke the silence and said, 'Tom, I want to say thank you. Thank you for arranging this evening specially so that you could tell me in person what is happening to you. You could as easily have told me on the phone and I appreciate you bringing me here to wine and dine at my favourite restaurant. You probably don't feel much like it right now!'

'There was absolutely no way I was going to tell you on the phone. I needed to see you and to be able to talk to you in person. I enjoy your company and you probably are the easiest person I know to be with, Nicola. You make me feel very relaxed and that's what I need right now.'

'I can assure you that the feeling is mutual,' said Nicola, looking around. 'Being here should make it easy to forget our troubles for a little while.'

'It's certainly got all the right ingredients for us to be happy – excellent food, good wine and a live band for us to dance the night away. What more could we ask!'

'I could ask if you are going to be all right, Tom!' said Nicola seriously. 'Because I don't know what I would do without you.'

'You're not going to have to do without me, I intend to be around for a long time. You've got to think positive, it's the only way,' said Tom as convincingly as he could, even if it was only to persuade Nicola that nothing was going to happen to him.

Tom got up from his bar stool and offered his arm to Nicola. 'Come on, let's go and eat and enjoy ourselves – the night is young and you are incredibly beautiful!'

'Flattery will get you everywhere!' said Nicola, climbing down from her bar stool and tucking her arm into Tom's. 'Right, lead the way!'

The restaurant manager saw them approaching the dining area and came up to welcome them. He showed them to a table by the window which Tom had reserved earlier in the day. As they sat down, Nicola looked at the view stretching across the River Thames and saw, in the darkness, all the lights shining in the buildings opposite and the lights from the passing boats sailing up and down the river.

'How popular those evening cruises have become,' she commented. 'It looks as if there are as many boats cruising along at night as you see in the daytime. It must be fun, cruising along, enjoying a nice meal and dancing on one of the decks. Have you ever tried it?'

'No, I haven't, but I'd like to give it a try. Let's promise to make it our first date together when I'm fully recovered and I need you to twirl me around the dance floor. Something to look forward to!'

5

The evening flew by all too quickly. They enjoyed an excellent dinner, accompanied by a claret chosen by Tom. Nicola said it was the nicest red wine that she could ever remember drinking. Tom was a connoisseur of wine and he had visited many of the vineyards in France. He had walked round the various plantations of grape vines, complete with a notebook and pencil, carefully jotting down any remarks that he needed to record for his future reference. Also, he had attended various lectures and wine tastings, so that he could come home with a real knowledge of the wines worth drinking. He eventually recommended them to his friends, who had never yet been disappointed with his choice.

Tom was glad he had decided to bring Nicola to The Riverbridge restaurant. It provided a great atmosphere, which was probably due to the fact that it was situated right by the river and the views looking across to the other side were spectacular. The lights now shone in the different buildings, including the Festival Hall, which was ablaze with light.

The dance band played to its usual high standard and both Tom and Nicola loved to dance. Tom was pleased to see Nicola relaxing as the evening wore on. When he had collected her from her home in Roehampton, he had been aware of how pale she seemed, but now she had the colour back in her cheeks and seemed totally relaxed. How she still remained married to a creep like Graham, Tom would never understand. Nicola was such a pretty woman, dark-haired, slim and with enormous blue eyes that lit up when she smiled. Her whole face became animated when she spoke and, if the truth be known, she was probably

Graham's biggest asset, but he didn't appreciate her, despite her being such a good wife and mother. Graham liked to complicate his life by running after different women and then, when he got what he wanted, he moved on to his next bit of excitement. Why he needed to behave like he did was beyond Tom's comprehension.

Tom looked across at Nicola's lovely face and knew that he would be more than happy to be married to her. She had that certain 'something' that he had never been able to find in any other woman, however hard he had tried. He guessed that Nicola, who knew of her husband's affairs, was just hiding behind a veneer.

'We seem to have spent most of our time talking about me, but I want to know how life is treating you, Nicky,' asked Tom somewhat apprehensively.

'I mustn't complain,' she replied. 'Marriage is full of problems, but I take one bite at a time. I'm kept pretty busy with the twins. I can't believe that they are sixteen and they should begin studying for their A-levels in September, for goodness sake! They both want to go on to university to study medicine.'

'That's great news, Nicky! Two doctors in one family, they must be very bright,' said Tom, knowing how proud Nicola would be feeling of her two offspring.

'Yes, they've always been good students and school work comes pretty easy to them. Also, my grandfather was a doctor, and his father before him, so I guess they've inherited their interest in medicine from them,' said Nicola, remembering her kindly grandfather and how much he was loved and admired by his patients.

'And what about you, Nicky? That's what the twins are doing, but I want to hear about your activities. Are you still playing golf and tennis? I know you are pretty good at both.' Tom was trying to find out what Nicola was doing without appearing intrusive.

'Yes, I play when I get the opportunity, but I've been working in the local library for the last few months. The head librarian had to leave through ill health, and I stepped in to help out while she recovers. I used to work in a school library, if you remember, and so I was approached as an obvious choice. But I'm enjoying it and I get to meet lots of people. The hours are good, too, and I can work around taking the twins to school and collecting them,' said Nicola, sipping her wine and enjoying the whole scene.

'Tell me to mind my own business, Nicky, but is Graham behaving himself at the time of going to press? Last time we met, you said he was staying away at night more and more and you were fed up to the teeth with the way he was treating you and the twins.'

Nicola thought for a short while before answering. 'Good question, Tom! The answer is, I'm not really sure. He seems very attentive towards us at the moment, but that could mean anything, and he's spending quite a bit of time at home when he's not on duty at the hotel. But sometimes in the past when he's been particularly attentive, it's been his guilty conscience coming to the fore. I've often thought that his naïvety borders on self-destruction.'

Tom laughed and said, 'That's a good way of putting it! As William Shakespeare used to say – "Thus conscience doth make cowards of us all". You would think that Graham had done with his roving by now!'

'Well, I don't want to think about it this evening, Tom, it's just nice to get away from everything and everyone for a little while and be myself. You mustn't worry about me. My life is all go and I certainly don't have too much time to dwell on my husband's indiscretions. Maybe I did when I was younger, but as I've got older, I've learnt to accept things as they are. All the worrying in the world won't change anything!'

'Come on, let's have another dance,' said Tom. He could sense that Nicola didn't want to talk any more about Graham and he would only have to guess at what she was really feeling, but he did know beyond any doubt that Nicola wasn't happy with her situation at home.

6

There was no question in Tom's mind, he definitely was feeling a great deal better after spending his evening with Nicola at The Riverbridge. She had that certain gift of being able to lift your spirits and help you forget your troubles for a while. Few people have this 'magic' but Nicola was certainly one of them.

When Tom took Nicola home, he saw her to her front door, but declined her offer for him to go inside for a coffee. Somehow, his relaxed and happy feeling would have evaporated and he knew that he would have tensed up knowing that Nicola's children and her mother were asleep upstairs. Tom didn't trust himself with Nicola; his feelings towards her were very strong and intense and he had no intention of putting himself in a compromising position. He was feeling anxious enough as it was, with the thought of his forthcoming operation looming up on the horizon, without getting emotionally worked up. It wouldn't be fair on himself or on Nicola.

Instead, he settled for a hug followed by a kiss on each cheek, but Nicola drew away very quickly and began searching in her handbag for her front door key. It was as if she too was in a hurry to get away, subduing her natural desires to be with Tom. He sensed it and he could feel a certain amount of tension during their parting.

'You must promise to let me know when you go in for your operation,' Nicola said with a kind of urgency. 'It goes without saying that I wish you all the luck in the world and that I'll be thinking about you.'

Tom replied. 'I'll telephone you as soon as I've got a date. You promise me that you will take care as well. You are a very special friend of mine and I want to see you happy!'

'Pigs might fly! Sorry, Tom, I shouldn't have said that. You mustn't worry about me, I can cope with all that life throws my way.' And with those words, Nicola turned her key in the latch, opened her front door and disappeared inside, closing the door quietly behind her.

Tom drove back to his home in Wimbledon Village. His feelings were a mixture of contentment and anxiety. The few hours he had spent in the company of Nicola had made him momentarily happy, but now that he was on his own once more and all the uncertainty and uneasiness were taking over.

There was so much he had wanted to say to Nicola but, as always, common sense had prevailed and he had decided against it. He had worked quite hard to keep the evening on a lighter note as it was his only way of coping with his emotions. Tom was surprised how, after all the years he had known Nicola, he still felt this strong, intense love towards her. It hadn't got him anywhere, but it certainly existed.

In the morning's post, Tom received a letter from his health insurers rejecting his claim for his heart bypass operation. Their reason for turning down the claim, was that they judged Tom to have a 'pre-existing' condition known as hyperlipidaemia, which had been excluded from the policy when Tom took it out with them.

Tom immediately telephoned Michael Pugh, his GP, and discussed the contents of the letter with him. As a result Dr Pugh confirmed that Tom was not suffering from hyperlipidaemia – which is when excessive amounts of fat deposits are found in a patient's bloodstream, causing a high cholesterol reading, which in turn leads to a blockage in the arteries.

'Tom, there's no way that you are suffering from hyperlipidaemia!' said Dr Pugh. 'You have got a genetic narrowing of your arteries. Anyway, you leave it with me and I'll get in touch with your insurers to sort it out, then I'll get back to you with some answers. In the meantime, remember what I said to you about the importance of remaining as fit as possible to minimize your recovery time.'

Tom thanked Michael Pugh for his much needed assurance and came away from the phone feeling a lot more confident. He went through from his study to the kitchen to make himself a mug of herbal tea – he would have preferred a large glass of his favourite claret, but decided against it because he was due to see a client in an hour's time. The tea made, he went back into his study and sat down to drink it in his armchair overlooking the garden.

He suddenly felt very tired. His late night was catching up with him and now he had the worry of the insurers refusing to pay for his operation. Tom thought that he would be going into hospital in the next couple of weeks and now he had received a total setback. He wondered how much easier it would be to cope if Nicola was there to support him, but he dismissed that thought as wishful thinking. But she would be able to give him all her love and support in his hour of need, of that he was quite certain.

For now, Tom had a lot of sorting out to do. His own workout sessions for a start, which Dr Pugh had said were so very necessary for his recovery, especially now that there would be the inevitable delay before he would be able to have his operation.

7

'But how are you going to be able to exercise without overdoing it?' asked Jane kindly as Tom put her through her weekly yoga and stretching routine.

It was a few days after his evening out with Nicola and Tom had felt more determined to approach his fitness regime, probably as a direct result of Nicola having lifted his spirits. His own secret longing to see her again was also high on his list of priorities.

Tom stopped demonstrating a particular stretch for Jane before saying, 'Well, Jane, the very first thing I've got to be aware of at all times is my chest. This means that I must never allow myself to exercise to the point where I experience any discomfort. So in order to raise my heart rate, I begin each workout session with a five-minute cycle ride or maybe a gentle walk. This in itself will automatically raise my heart beat and it will gradually warm up the deeper muscles in my body. I then do a series of short stretches to make sure that my joints have been put through their full range of movement and all the major muscles are worked. I'm ready then to do some form of aerobic exercise, which I usually do for about twenty minutes.'

'It sounds good to me!' said Jane. 'It reminds me of the old saying "Physician heal thyself". Looking on the plus side, you'll certainly be in a marvellous position to advise any of your clients who have either suffered a stroke or had a bypass operation. I'm a great believer that everything in your life happens for a good reason. You probably have to go through all this so that you can help and understand others. I've discovered for myself that I can now listen and feel for fellow cancer sufferers. I don't have to guess at what they feel – I know!'

'It's certainly a great learning curve,' said Tom. 'For example, I know that I mustn't let my heart beat exceed 120 to 130 beats per minute. Any discomfort begins at around 150 bpm, so now wearing a heart-rate monitor is a must for me. I make sure that I keep the rate more than 100 bpm, but I won't allow it to go much higher.'

'Clever stuff!' said Jane, smiling. 'All I can say is, that it's a good job that you know what you're doing. Personally, I'd feel more than a little nervous jumping around knowing that I've got all this blockage going on inside me. Do be careful, not to overdo it.'

'You mustn't worry about me, Jane, I know exactly what I'm doing and just how far I can go! I just wish I could get into hospital and get the whole thing over and done with,' said Tom, who was feeling the stress of his situation even more than he dared admit. It had turned out to be one long waiting game.

Jane knew Tom well enough to know that he was putting up a good show of bravado, but she could sense his anxiety and he couldn't fool her, she was much too long in the tooth. The fact that Tom's private medical insurers had refused to pay for his operation and hospital stay must have knocked him for six.

'What's to be your next move regarding your operation?' she asked.

'Well, now that I know I can't get it done privately, I'll have to have it done on the NHS. It just means a longer wait, and instead of a private hospital it will be an NHS one. But I'm more than thankful that it is the same surgeon who is going to perform the op. I'm afraid it's the same thing, "different gravy", so to speak!'

Jane smiled to herself; there Tom went again, trying to make light of it all! She also realized what a very disciplined character he was.

Later on in the day, Tom was sitting at his desk in the study, writing up progress reports for his different clients.

He was so absorbed in what he was doing that the shrill ring of the telephone literally made him jump. Tom picked up the receiver. '462794 – Tom Dunn speaking.'

'Hi, Tom!' The familiar voice of his friend sounded down the wire.

'Hello, David! Great minds think alike. I intended to give you a call when I'd finished my reports, but you've beaten me to it.'

'I wondered if you were free this evening to have a pub supper with me? We could meet at The Fox and Grapes – I need to reminisce with you,' said David.

'That sounds fine with me. I'll meet you in the pub at seven thirty. What's with the reminiscing bit? The mind boggles!' said Tom, and laughed. He and David had spent so much time with each other over the years and shared in so many good and bad times that it was hard for Tom to guess which one David wished to remember.

'I've been asked by a fellow editor to do a series of articles for a monthly yachting magazine under the heading of "Narrow Escapes" and I thought an appropriate one would be to write about the time we had when we sailed from Rotterdam to Brighton. It was all pretty hair-raising stuff, and that's putting it mildly!'

'It was a terrifying experience, David! At one point I rather thought we wouldn't live to tell the tale! I'll be more than happy to spend the evening secure in our local, enjoying a good meal and a glass of wine, whilst conjuring up our eventful voyage.'

'Right then. Thanks, Tom. I'll see you this evening, complete with my notepad and pen!'

'I'll look forward to it! 'Bye for now,' said Tom, replacing the receiver.

David had been an editor of a boating and yachting magazine for as long as Tom had known him. There wasn't much David didn't know about boating or writing. He had gone into the world of journalism straight after leaving university and had done extremely well for himself.

8

Tom decided to walk from his home in the village to the pub on the common. It was only a mile or so away and he had no need to take the car and run the risk of being breathalysed on his way back. That stress he could well do without and he enjoyed walking, especially on a clear evening such as this. The Fox and Grapes was probably a twenty-five minute brisk walk from door to door. Tom wanted to enjoy his wine with a meal, possibly followed by a cognac or two!

It was a dark, dry, cool evening as Tom made his way over the common, passing the pond and noticing how still it appeared now the daytime activities had finished. It wasn't the usual hive of activity with dogs being walked, children feeding the ducks and couples strolling hand in hand enjoying each other's company. At night it all seemed a little spooky. The trees were stationary, the pond was silent and dark and it seemed as if he had the common to himself, apart from a few cars passing by on the surrounding roads with their headlights on, but they were quite a distance away. Tom saw the lights on in the pub as he approached it and they proved a welcoming sight in the darkness.

As Tom entered the bar, he immediately felt the atmosphere of this country pub engulf him and it was a warm, homely feeling. He saw David at one of the small round tables and he made his way over to him. By now the pub was pretty full with people drinking, eating, talking and generally unwinding after their day's work. They had chosen this friendly pub in which to spend their evening and to relax from the cares of the day.

'Hi, David, it's good to see you!' said Tom. 'I'm not late, am I?'

'No, it's me who's early. What will you have to drink?' replied David, getting up from his chair to get their orders in.

'A glass of red wine, please,' replied Tom. 'Do you mind bringing the menu back with the drinks and then we can choose our meal, before we get down to the serious business of reminiscing.'

'Will do. I'm looking forward to it. I've got my pen and pad at the ready!'

Armed with their drinks and the meal ordered, both men sat back comfortably in their chairs. David rested his notepad on his lap. 'I've decided to head my article "GAINING MY OCEAN GOING MASTER'S CERTIFICATE IN MY 33 FOOT SLOOP – UNDER DIFFICULTY!"'

'You can say that again!' said Tom, and laughed. 'You were already a very competent sailor, but I remember that you needed this qualification to sail the Atlantic. The guy who came along from the Royal Yachting Association to examine you certainly wouldn't have had a clue what he was letting himself in for!'

'Poor devil!' replied David. 'But, equally, neither did you, or my cousin Mike, or his son Richard. When I invited the three of you to be my crew, you all enthusiastically accepted, You probably just imagined an interesting sail from Rotterdam over to England, not the adventure that lay ahead of us!'

Tom said, 'It was all part of life's rich pattern. It certainly got my adrenalin working overtime and gave us a real taste of life on the high seas.'

'When the examiner, Alec, asked me to prepare the route plan with tides, weather, etc., it all seemed pretty straightforward – it was when it was all put into practice that it went crazy! I can remember us setting off from Rotterdam at dawn and sailing into the North Sea. Then we made for Fécamp, which took about twenty hours.'

'Yes, and I recall the sea was very choppy and I was

conscious of the sound of creaking wood while we tossed and rolled about,' said Tom, feeling somewhat smug that he was now sitting warm and safe in the pub. 'The watch worked well, with us changing over every six to eight hours. The "hot bunking" system we adopted should most definitely be put in your article – I'm sure it would interest your readers.' (Hot bunking is when the members of the crew have been on watch and are ready to change over. They are very cold and in wet clothes and are very tired, but they make tea for the next people who are going on watch. They wake the next guys up, give them tea and say, 'You are on watch in ten minutes!' They drink their tea in their bunks, while the crew on watch take off their oilskins and thick top pullover, which they then put on. The new men on watch are consequently kitted out in warm clothes and the old watch in turn climb into the warm bunks for their sleep.)

'I agree,' replied David. He knew that Tom would remember all the details of their trip and add some human interest to his forthcoming article.

'Yes and "hot bunking" really works well, doesn't it? Without that way of changing over the watch, I expect we would be freezing, especially at night time. We made very good time to Wissant, that little town on the French coast, remember, and as I changed watch, so the tide changed, and so did the wind,' said Tom, looking down at the generous fillet steak and French fries that the waitress had just placed before him.

'There's just so much that I could write about, Tom!' said David, tucking into a plateful of ham and eggs with real gusto. 'But seeing that it's an article they're after, we will have to keep it fairly short. Pity really, I think I could write a book about that particular trip!'

9

'I really enjoyed that!' said Tom. 'They certainly know how to cook a steak, which is more than I can say for a lot of restaurants I have eaten in. In fact, I've still got room for some of their home-baked apple pie and ice cream. How about you?'

'Sounds like a good idea to me. I'll go and order two portions and some more drinks. Your impending operation has certainly not damaged your appetite!'

'Great, isn't it?' said Tom, and laughed. 'Sometimes, I even forget that it's all going to happen. An evening spent like this, it all seems a million miles away and I really do feel fine.'

'Well, it just proves how very fit you are. You're probably in a better position than most to cope with it – the average person is pretty unfit and possibly overweight. I'll just go over to the bar and then we'll resume our memoirs.'

Tom watched David walk over to the bar and then lean against it, waiting to put their order in. He realized that the letter from the hospital could arrive any day now and he was savouring the feeling of being able to spend quality time with his friend. All the pleasurable things in life would have to be put on hold after the serious operation which was facing him.

'Right!' said David, putting a large glass of port in front of Tom. 'Where did we get to in our saga?'

'Let's take it from when we were heading for Cherbourg,' replied Tom. 'It was then that we realized that the ship's log wasn't working and the instruments hadn't moved to disclose the nautical miles. I remember you sending Richard over the side into the icy water with a rope tied around his waist. We thought that the log had jammed, but in actual fact it had dropped off!'

'It was at that point that I took the decision to sail straight to Brighton to a yard where I could get the ship's log repaired. I imagined that the Channel would be all right at night, as we had plenty of fuel and the forecast was good. But just as the sun set, so the wind dropped. We managed to keep under sail for a while, but were unable to make the required speed. I decided to start the engine, and then I realized there was damage at the bottom of the boat and that sea water was now mixed in with the fuel. This damage to the boat's bottom had obviously been done when I had a little scrape in the waterways of Holland!' recalled David, who was making copious notes, as well as talking.

'Yes,' said Tom. 'It was at this stage that we realized that we had no log, no wind and no engine! Luckily, we did have batteries, so we were able to have the navigation lights on as we drifted through the busiest waterway in the world at night. Unfortunately for us, the batteries failed after three hours and so our navigation lights went out!'

'No log, no wind, no engine, no lights!' David said, remembering only too well that he had considered putting out a 'Mayday' call, but had chosen not to and decided to risk the rest of the voyage.

'Do you remember how we saw those enormous tankers? They were huge, black and silent as we drifted in between them. I guess that is the stuff that nightmares are made of!' Tom could picture the vastness and blackness of them to this day.

'Yes, I remember,' replied David. 'We had the sail up at that stage and shone the torches up, so if the lookouts weren't asleep, they would see our sail. But, no joy, they didn't see us!'

'What about that tanker with the set of lights up that we didn't recognize? We looked it up in a reference manual and it said "ship out of control – steering not working"! It would have been kinder not to have looked it up!'

'However, we survived to tell our tale! We weaved in and

out of those wretched tankers and then as dawn broke, the wind got up and we went full sail heading for Brighton. We then had yet another hazard to deal with as Brighton Marina is very tricky to get into. You have to move from side to side while going forward in and out of the harbour wall, so, if you remember, we were forced to take the sails down. We had no engine, so it was a question of judging our speed from the sails to get us up into the harbour mouth in order to tie up to the jetty. If the speed had proved to be too fast, we would have crashed into the other boats in the jetty. But, as we sit here eating our delicious supper and drinking our wine, and preparing my article, I guess I managed to get that required speed just right.'

Tom sat back and applauded. 'That was great, David! I even felt the adrenalin pumping again at the thought of it all! I'm sure your writing will be a great success.'

'I hope they'll like it, and thanks for your help in its preparation, not to mention all the excellent crewing you did for me at the time,' said David sincerely.

'I just have one favour to ask of you, David.'

'Fire away.'

'Don't ask me to do any crewing for you in my convalescent period – I'd much rather not, if you don't mind!'

10

It was sheer magic! Totally unexpected, but it created a feeling of unadulterated happiness.

Tom was spending the day up in London and was killing a bit of time before his appointment by looking around Covent Garden. He was fascinated by the shops, the market, the street entertainers and everything and everybody who made up the world of that truly unique place.

He heard some music being played, followed by applause, and walked over to a balcony which overlooked a courtyard full of people sitting around little tables, drinking coffees or cold drinks – a very continental scene. The reason for the enthusiastic clapping was a group of young musicians playing their violins in one corner of the courtyard below. Tom joined the other people who were already leaning over the wooden railings of the balcony, listening and watching the scene being acted out below.

The musicians, six of them, each dressed casually in jeans and shirts, some wearing trainers, some sandals, were playing their violins as if their very lives depended upon them. They announced that they were now going to play the 'William Tell Overture' and then, with a rhythmic stamping of their feet, they set the music going.

Tom watched them intently, leaning his elbows on the balcony rail and looking down enthralled. A little girl in a pink dress with matching pink shoes, who couldn't have been more than three years old, left her mother at their table and toddled over to one of the musicians and proceeded to stare up at her, all the while bobbing up and down to the music. The violinist quickly became aware of this little one watching her and bent herself down to her level, continuing to play her violin all the time. Probably in her early twenties, she was making her violin literally sing! For a short time, it seemed as though she was playing entirely for the little girl's benefit, oblivious to everyone else who was listening and watching, and Tom thought it was a wonderful sight to witness. He was aware of feeling carefree and cheerful and his troubles seemed a million miles away at this moment in time.

When they had finished playing the overture, a young woman came round to the spectators, holding out a cloth cap and asking if they would like to put some cash in it for the players. Tom didn't hesitate and put a handful of change willingly into the hat and said, 'What a truly wonderful group! May I ask who they are?'

The girl smiled broadly before answering. 'They are students from the Royal College of Music. This morning we had an opera singer to entertain the visitors.'

'Well, they play superbly and I consider it a privilege to listen to our future musicians – thank you!'

'And thank you, sir! Enjoy the rest of your day.' The girl said before moving on to the next group of observers with her hat.

Tom felt as though he had entered another world, nothing else existed but what was happening right now. It was an effort to tear himself away from the balcony and force himself back into reality.

The reason for his visit to London was to meet up with his family solicitor at his offices in Albemarle Street, a stone's throw from Marble Arch. Tom had deliberately made a day of it because he had wanted to have lunch with an ex-colleague who now worked in offices in the Strand. Tom had met Antony when they worked for a computer firm together out in Germany for five years, a very happy period of Tom's life. When they had completed their job, Tom had taken the decision to have a complete change of career and had trained to become a personal fitness trainer. A far cry from the world of computers, but something he had always wanted to do.

Tom and Antony had met in the plush bar of the Waldorf Hotel and then lunched in the hotel's equally grand restaurant. A stroll afterwards into Covent Garden had been an obvious choice for Tom, while Antony had made his way back to his office. He had been shocked to learn of Tom's condition, but, like all of Tom's friends, Antony had offered encouragement and sympathy, tinged with disbelief that it could happen to someone as fit as Tom.

Tom hailed a taxi and asked the driver to take him to Albemarle Street. Twenty minutes later, he was being shown into George Scott's office.

George could not be described as a typical solicitor. He was a nice-looking man, in his fifties, well dressed and with a warm and friendly manner. He was efficient, but he never came across as patronizing, as many solicitors do. George stood up when his secretary showed Tom into his room and came over to meet him.

'It's good to see you, Tom!' said George, shaking Tom's hand firmly before going back to his chair. 'Please sit yourself down. Would you like a cup of tea or maybe a coffee? Sorry I couldn't see you before four o'clock, but it's been like a madhouse here, with several of my colleagues off sick.'

'The time is fine with me, no worries,' replied Tom, relaxing into a comfortable chair facing George across his large impressive leather desk. 'In fact, I've taken a day off and spent it in London, lunching with a friend at the Waldorf, followed by a look around Covent Garden, and, yes please, I would like some tea!'

George rang through to his secretary and asked her to bring them both some tea.

11

George stirred the sugar into his cup of tea slowly and said, 'I was distressed to read the contents of your letter to me, and I can quite understand you wanting to put your house in order before going in for your operation. I've got your file here with your last will you made in 1979. Maybe you need only to add a couple of codicils rather than making a complete new one.'

'No, George, I'd rather make a new one. Life changes, circumstances change and I did make that last will twenty years ago. A lot of water has gone under the bridge since then and I don't imagine a couple of codicils could cover my requests. My surgeon has been very honest and open with me and has gone to great lengths to spell out the plus and minus sides of my operation. Evidently, the success rate is high in bypass operations, but there is always the risk that the patient could have a stroke while on the operating table or even die. You will gather that I have a very open and sincere man in whose hands I'm placing my life! On the bright side, if all goes according to plan, I should be back in harness in about three months' time.'

'I quite understand,' said George, silently thanking God that he himself was not having to face Tom's ordeal. 'Tell me what you want and who you want to be your executors, and then I can draft it out and send you a copy for your approval.'

Without one moment's hesitation, Tom replied, 'I would like Nicola Ross and you to be the executors of my will and Nicola will also be my main beneficiary.'

'Do I know the lady in question?' asked George, trying, without success, to recall the name.

'No, you don't, I keep her well under wraps,' replied Tom with a broad grin. 'She is my dearest friend. She makes me feel good and I love everything about her.'

'This lady sounds to me as though she ought to be your wife rather than your best friend. What's the problem?' asked George, who by now was becoming somewhat intrigued.

'I'm afraid she's married, more's the pity. But what is so upsetting to me is that she is married to a cad, a real womanizer. He has cheated on Nicola for nearly all her married life. I often wonder how she stomachs it all, but the plus side to the marriage is that they have two wonderful children – twins – a boy and a girl of sixteen and she idolizes them. It's the twins who have kept her marriage alive and I know that for a fact, because I've seen the way she is with them and how they worship their mother. It's a sad case, but I'm quite sure it's not unique,' said Tom, realizing how much he had been able to tell George without any embarrassment at all. It was good to be able to talk, knowing full well that it was all in complete confidence. George had been a good friend to Tom over the years as well as proving an excellent family solicitor. George was definitely from the old school and Tom had great respect for him.

'So how do you fit into this set-up, Tom? After all, you are just about to make Nicola the chief beneficiary of your very considerable estate,' said George, thinking that Tom was obviously in some kind of emotional dilemma.

'Good question, George!' said Tom. 'I can't really explain it. I told her many years ago that I was willing to be anything she wanted – her husband, her lover or just a friend – and she chose my friendship. That's not what I really want, but as long as she knows that I am always there for her, that's fine by me. I'd rather have friendship than nothing, and so that is what I have had to settle for, and what happens in the future is all in the lap of the gods.'

'She must be some lady! You have always had your head screwed on so firmly and you have always given me the impression that you know exactly what you want out of life. I must admit that I have wondered why you never married, though. You have so much to offer a woman, but now I can quite see why I've never received an invitation to your wedding. And how has Nicola reacted to your bypass operation?' asked George kindly.

'She takes everything in her stride, but I can tell she's worried by the way she reacted to my news. But you see, George, she's given me the really deep feeling of wanting to get better and get back to normal. I just know that I need to be there for her to pick up the pieces,' said Tom, and George knew that Tom meant every word he said.

The rest of their time together was spent drawing up all the details of Tom's new will.

12

A week later Tom had received his will, signed it and returned it to George for its safe keeping. He felt relieved that he had 'put his house in order' just in case; Tom didn't want any loose ends left. He had always been a great organizer and had an exceptionally tidy and orderly mind.

Two weeks later, Tom received a letter offering him a bed at a large NHS hospital for his bypass operation. Fortunately, it was still to be performed by the surgeon whom Tom had seen privately, and for this Tom was more than thankful. He had liked and trusted the specialist, who had taken the trouble to explain at great length the benefits as well as the risks of this very serious operation. He was a straightforward kind of man – Tom's kind of man – in whose hands he was just about to put his life.

Tom felt very alone when he read his admission letter. Most things happen to you with family and friends, but with his forthcoming operation coming up, he felt entirely alone. Nobody could actually have the operation for him and emotions came flooding into his mind. It was a strange sensation and it produced a well of loneliness into the whole of his being. Tom also felt a great need to telephone Nicola to share his feelings with her but he decided against it. He knew it would add to his and her already troubled feelings. However, as he had promised he would, he phoned her later on in the day to let her know his admission date.

Tom waited with his heart thumping loudly in his chest for Nicola to answer the telephone. It seemed to take forever before he heard the familiar voice – the voice he loved so much.

'Richmond 649646. Nicola Ross speaking!'

'Hi, Nicky! It's Tom.'

'Tom! I was just thinking about you and wondering how you are and whether you had heard anything yet. Talk about telepathy!'

'That's the very reason for my call,' replied Tom, who was more than a little relieved that it was Nicola who had picked up the receiver.

'You've heard then? When's it going to be?' she asked anxiously.

'There's a bed for me on Monday and they are going to operate first thing on Tuesday morning. The sooner the better, as far as I'm concerned. The waiting has been somewhat stressful, as you can imagine!'

'I can indeed,' replied Nicola tenderly and then added, 'Tom, please can I be the one to take you in? I want to be there with you.'

Tom was totally unprepared for Nicola's offer and replied, 'Thanks, Nicky! I'd like nothing more than for you drive me to the hospital, but surely you'll be driving the twins to school? I have to be there for nine o'clock.'

'That's no problem. I'll ask my mother to take them to school on Monday. As I said, I want to be there with you. It's a hell of an ordeal you're facing and you'll need all the support you can get,' she said with a catch in her voice which certainly didn't go undetected by Tom.

'Well, that's fine with me just so long as I'm not putting you to any trouble. Can you be here by seven thirty? I don't want to be late after all my waiting!'

'No problem,' replied Nicola. 'I'll be with you around seven o'clock. Take care, Tom, and remember that I need you to be around for a very long time yet!'

'The feeling is mutual, darling, I promise you! And thanks for offering to take me to hospital. I appreciate it more than you know. I'll see you on Monday morning then – at least that gives me something to look forward to. 'Bye for now,' said Tom, and hung up quickly before his emotions got the better of him. He was feeling very vulnerable now that his operation was only a few days away. To have been told by Nicola that she needed him made him feel all the more determined to get through this wretched operation, and he continued to sit by the telephone for quite a while, wondering which one of them needed the other the most.

13

Monday dawned. Tom looked at the clock on his bedside table and saw it was only four thirty. He lay in bed knowing only too well that there was pretty well no hope of his getting back to sleep. Today was the day!

His thoughts instinctively turned to Nicola. He would be seeing her in roughly three hours' time and his longing for her was as intense as ever. He remembered yet again their one night alone in a mountain refuge in the French Alps. He remembered that night as if it was yesterday, and he could picture every detail of it. How he had taken Nicola into his arms and laid her gently down onto the rug in front of the roaring fire, which he had made in order to warm them up. How they had loved each other that night. All barriers were down, the rest of the world had been blotted out and there had just been the two of them; no one else existed. Both of them knew that night what they really meant to each other. Their lovemaking had been perfect, their bodies and their very souls had been locked together for those few precious hours. It was only reality that had stopped them the next day, and all the other people came back into their lives. How they had wished it could have been different, but life goes on and their night together as lovers would have to remain a treasured memory.

Tom got out of bed, showered and dressed and then went downstairs to his study. He had already packed his bag for his hospital stay, and so he sat down at his desk and read through a few letters and reports. He checked that his clients' sessions had all been covered by his able team of trainers while he was out of action. He smiled to himself, thinking how some of them would get along together. It really was a very personal thing to keep people fit and, more often than not, Tom had become a confidant to them, especially to the ladies. He didn't complain, as he felt that personal fitness and peace of mind went hand in hand.

The study felt cold and Tom lent over and switched the electric fire on to heat the room up. He put the chill of the room down to nerves, it was all part and parcel of the anticipation he was experiencing. He longed for the next few weeks to be over and done with, so that he could then go forward and get on with the rest of his life.

After what seemed an eternity, Tom heard the sound of Nicola's car drawing up on to his driveway. He heard the engine stop and then the sound of her car door shutting, followed by her footsteps approaching the front door and finally the ringing of his door bell.

He opened the door wide and automatically held his arms open to Nicola in greeting. 'Nicola, it's so very good to see you! Come on inside, and I'll make you a coffee. We don't need to leave here for another twenty minutes at least.'

'Well, if you're sure. I know I'm a little early, but I didn't want you fretting that you'd be late getting to hospital. That's the last thing you need,' replied Nicola, who was still embracing him. Reluctantly she released her arms from around him and made her way into the kitchen.

Tom had already boiled the kettle just in case, and now he poured them each a mugful.

'Tom, how are you feeling? Tell me the truth. What were you thinking about before I arrived? Are you very nervous?' Nicola spoke quickly, hardly pausing for breath, both hands clasping her mug.

'Hey, hold on, Nicky! One question at a time, if you don't mind!' said Tom.

'Sorry, I always talk too fast when I'm nervous. Anyone would think that I'm the one who's going to be operated on! My tummy's been doing somersaults ever since I woke up this morning.'

'Mine too!' replied Tom. 'But the waiting's been awful

and now I'm relieved that I can get on with it. In answer to your question what was I thinking about before you arrived, the answer is quite simply, you!'

'Oh, Tom, please don't let anything happen to you – I couldn't bear to spend the rest of my life without you! You are my dearest friend, my rock to lean on. It has always helped knowing that you are just a phone call away.' Nicola put her coffee down and walked over to where Tom was sitting. She placed her arms around him and for a few precious moments held his head to her breast.

14

Tom was admitted to a large ward consisting of thirty beds, where most of the patients were being treated for their malfunctioning heart or lungs. At first glance, it reminded Tom of pictures he'd seen of Victorian hospital wards. By each bed was a locker and above the bed there was a light and what looked like tubes with an oxygen mask dangling on the end. It all looked very sparse and eerie. Tom went on to learn that a lot of the patients' problems had been brought about due to excessive smoking. It had obviously been a question of 'live now, pay later', but it had become a harsh reality to have to pay for it with ruined health and, at worst, their lives.

Once settled into the ward, clad in pyjamas and dressing gown, Tom sat up on his bed and started to read his book. One of his clients had recently had a trilogy published – a family saga – and it seemed a good opportunity to read the story now that he had been grounded. Tom smiled to himself after reading the first couple of chapters; he could just imagine Sue saying to him, 'Well, Tom, what did you think?' She had given the books to him as a 'get well' gift and said that she would value his opinion of them – good or bad! But she had added, 'Just as long as you don't say "Rubbish!"'

Tom's specialist came in to see him, as did the anaesthetist, and they went through tomorrow's procedure with him. The nursing team kept him busy and carried out various tests on him, with all the questions that had to be asked and noted down for the records. So Monday passed by very quickly and his reading of Sue's book was constantly interrupted, but it had helped. The very fact he knew the author well and trained her out on a weekly basis made reading the book more fun.

The night time didn't prove so good. Tom was aware of all the coughing, choking, spluttering and wheezing of his fellow patients and it all sounded pretty loud. The ward lights had been dimmed right down so patients could sleep, but the sound effects were pretty awful.

A nurse came round at 6.30 a.m. on Tuesday with a 'wake-up' call, but Tom was already very wide awake. The nurse took his blood pressure reading and his temperature and confirmed that he was the first patient to go down to theatre, so there would be no hanging around today. This was 'D-day' and, strangely enough, Tom didn't feel nervous, he felt relaxed and ready for his operation. He had complete confidence in his surgeon's skill and that of the anaesthetist, and that helped him to relax.

After being given his pre-med, Tom was wheeled down to the anaesthetic room. He was quite light-headed and felt no tension at all. Everything and everybody seemed so far away.

The next thing that Tom remembered was waking up in his bed, back in the ward. When he first opened his eyes, it took him a little time to register where he was. There was a nurse standing by his side, busy taking his blood pressure, and she said, 'It's all over, Mr Dunn! You've had your operation and you are now in the intensive care ward. We will be keeping you here for the next twenty-four hours.'

'I could have sworn I was back in the ward they took me to the theatre from,' replied Tom, lifting the oxygen mask away from his mouth so that he could speak.

'No, you're in here now, Mr Dunn, as we need to monitor you all the time. You've got tubes and drips attached to you, which is normal post-operative procedure, and there'll be a nurse close to you always, to cope with any blip that might occur. You're in safe hands, I promise you!'

The next few days became somewhat of a blur in Tom's memory, as he drifted in and out of sleep. At the waking times, the nursing staff and physiotherapists got him out of bed and mobile. Tom was well aware of all the tubes and wires which were attached to his body and his extensive wounds. There was a large cut from under his throat, which extended down his chest and stopped at his waist line. An equally long incision had been made on the inside of his left arm, where the surgeon had taken an artery, and another incision had been made down his right leg, where a vein had been removed. The surgeon had used the artery and the vein to replace the blocked ones in his chest.

Throughout his stay in hospital, Tom's desire to get better was boosted by the visits he received from Nicola and all the encouragement and love she gave so willingly to him.

Long after his surgery, Tom remembered how her visits had really helped his recovery. She had possibly been the main person who had made his ordeal just that little bit easier to bear and he never forgot that she had said, 'Tom, you're my dearest friend! You've always been there for me along life's path, in the good times and the bad. I can promise you that I, in turn, will be there for you!'

Tom thought how very much he loved this woman. He loved everything about her: the way she looked, the way she talked, the way she smiled and laughed, the way she dressed. The only thing he didn't like was the fact that she was married to that two-timing cad, Graham Ross.

15

Tom looked around at the majesty of the Canadian Rockies and he liked what he saw. The sights were magnificent and his surroundings all added to his longing for Nicola's presence, It almost hurt him physically and he felt that familiar well of loneliness stir within him. He thought how wonderful it would be to share the awesome sights of the Rockies with her. Why did she have to be the unobtainable woman in his life? Tom knew for certain that she wasn't happy with Graham, but he also knew her situation well enough, and there was no way that she would voluntarily leave him. Part of Nicola was very Victorian and she believed that her children needed both their real father and mother to bring them up in a secure environment. Over the years, Nicola had heard and witnessed too many sad stories of children who had become victims of broken homes and she had no intention of adding her two to the ever increasing list.

It was five thirty in the morning and the sun was beginning to rise over the glacier which faced Tom's bedroom window. Chateau Lake Louise was the nearest place he had ever been to Heaven on this earth! The mountains, with their peaks covered in snow, came down to the shores of the lake. The Chateau was at one end and an enormous mountain at the other, covered with a glacier. The glacier reminded Tom of a large wedding cake with a great slice cut out of it. The bare rock looked like dark fruit and the deep layer of snow on top was the icing sugar. The lower sides of the mountains around the lake were covered with fir trees. Everything was very still at this early hour and the lake resembled a mirror. Tom watched from his bedroom window as the sun slowly turned the snow pink as it rose slowly from behind the mountains. The lake turned a beautiful shade of deep turquoise and Tom could feel a lump rise in his throat. He felt very privileged to witness the sights before him. He could well imagine how many authors and artists had been inspired to write about or paint this spectacular sunrise.

If ever in the future he had the chance to take Nicola somewhere very special, without a doubt it would be here that he would bring her. Tom had an overwhelming desire to telephone Nicola in England right now, but he decided against his need, as more likely than not, it would be Graham who would answer his call. Then the magic would be well and truly lost.

Tom looked at his watch; the snow was getting whiter by the minute and the sky was as blue as could be. What was the point of wishful thinking – life was to be lived and it was a negative feeling to be wishing for the unobtainable.

Tom had made an excellent recovery from his operation, which was now a comfortable three months behind him. He had come over to Canada at the invitation of his friends James and Judi, who lived in Vancouver. They had planned this trip to the Rockies and had very kindly insisted that Tom came along with them; it would be a convalescent holiday for him. James had been at school with Tom and, despite living out in Canada, had always kept in contact with him. Judi was a Canadian girl who had met James on a business trip and they had fallen in love and married within six months of their first meeting. They both worked for an international bank which had branches all over the world, including England and Canada. Judi had persuaded James to live in Vancouver after they married and he had never regretted it. James loved life in Canada and, more important, he loved his wife.

James and Judi knew only to well of Tom's passion for mountains, as James had been on ski trips with Tom to Switzerland and Austria. Each trip, Tom had been the leader and the ski instructor. Now it seemed the most obvious thing to invite Tom along with them to explore the Rockies. Tom hadn't hesitated in accepting their generosity and was enjoying seeing all the beauty that surrounded them.

Yesterday, they had visited the Athabasca Glacier on the Columbia Icefield. They had boarded a snow-coach, which the driver steered down a thirty-two-degree incline on to the surface of the glacier. The snow-coach had enormous wheels with massive thick tyres in order for it to grip the ice and Tom and his friends found actually walking on the glacier a unique experience. The driver of the coach, Dean, also doubled up as the guide and he gave a really amusing commentary to the visitors, ending the visit by giving everyone a drink of icy water from a fast-flowing stream. This water had melted from ice that had fallen as snow up to one hundred and fifty years ago and it is the purest natural water known. Somehow, Tom found this fact really incredible and he savoured every mouthful of water in that cheap plastic cup. He thought a cut-glass goblet would have been much more appropriate!

Tom watched as a party of people worked on the glacier, complete with a camera crew, and was informed that they were from the *Reader's Digest*, preparing an article on glaciers for their readers.

'Well,' said Tom to James, 'they couldn't get any better information than being right here on the glacier – what a fantastic location to be sent to! I'll look out for the issue that's got the write-up in when I get back home and I'll send you a copy.'

16

To capture the beauty and the majesty of the Canadian Rockies, James had decided to go by coach and train. He had had various reports from friends who had done the trip and they had all been good.

Tom had flown out from London Heathrow to Calgary and had met James and Judi in one of the large hotels there, which was where the coach would pick them up for their journey. Going by coach ensured that they would have an experienced driver and guide with them throughout their holiday and, as it was only for a week, they wanted to make the most of their time. The trip would take them from Calgary to Banff, Lake Louise, Jasper Park, Vancouver Island and finally Vancouver.

There was so much to see in this one week that Tom swore by the end of it that he was suffering from visual indigestion!

One evening as they were sitting enjoying their dinner at the Jasper Park Lodge overlooking yet another magnificent lake, Tom said, 'I really want to thank you guys for asking me along on this fantastic trip. To me it's been a trip of a lifetime – just what the doctor ordered – and I can honestly say that I feel totally relaxed, despite the roll that we've been kept on!'

'You can say that again!' said Judi, smiling. 'It's amazing how much we've managed to see and do in the last few days. Sometimes it's been a bit of a sweat having to have our suitcases out of our rooms by seven, but it's all been worth it. We can catch up on sleep when we get back home again! I do hope that all this travelling and living out of suitcases hasn't been too much for you, Tom. After all that you've been through, it's not exactly been what you would describe as a relaxing holiday!'

'No problem, Judi!' replied Tom, who felt touched by Judi's genuine concern for his well being. 'I've enjoyed every minute and we've spent a lot of the time sitting in the coach being driven by Steve and listening to an amusing commentary by Todd – what more could we ask!'

'I'm finding it hard to take in all that we're seeing,' said James. 'The Canadian Rockies must have some of the most beautiful landscapes on earth. There's a fantastic new sight around every bend and twist in the road. I already want to come back for more and we've not even gone home yet!'

'I know exactly how you're feeling,' said Tom. 'Sometimes it's a real drag to have to leave a place and get back on the coach again. I felt it the most when we left Chateau Lake Louise. Time seemed to stand stiil while I was there and I had this huge desire to climb that mountain right opposite my bedroom window. All my old longings to climb mountains and to ski down them came flooding back, but goodness knows when I'll be doing anything as adventurous as that again.'

'At the rate you're progressing, I guess that time isn't too far off,' said Judi. 'You've advanced so much in such a very short space of time, and it only goes to prove just how fit you were before having your op.' Judi admired the way that Tom had coped with major surgery and then got on with his life. He was such a positive person and if there was anything bothering him, he certainly didn't complain.

They arrived at Jasper Park Lodge at about four o'clock, giving them ample time to look around and explore the lovely grounds. Jasper Park was made up of a complex of log cabins set in the gardens around the lake. Each guest was allocated one of the cabins for their night's stay and Tom's was alongside Judi and James's. Tom had been busy unpacking his holdall when Judi had appeared at his back door.

'Tom, you've just got to go over to the window by your front door and take a look outside!'

Tom stopped what he was doing and went out of his bedroom through to the hall. He was wondering what Judi was getting so excited about but when he looked, he wasn't disappointed. For there, grazing outside on the lawn, were two elks and their baby. What a sight! Another vision to add to his Canadian memory bank. And how he would have loved to have shared it all with that certain lady named Nicola!

17

Tom and Judi were taking a walk down by the lake the following morning after breakfast, whilst James had gone off with his camera to photograph as much of Jasper Park Lodge as possible.

They had been walking for about half an hour, admiring this fantastic lake, complete with manicured lawns which led down to its edge. They also had their first encounter with the famous Canada geese, who were sitting or strutting around on the lawns.

Judi stopped suddenly in her tracks, turned to Tom and said, 'Tom, would you mind if I asked you a very personal question?'

'Not at all, Judi. Fire away!' replied Tom, wondering what on earth she was about to come up with.

'Well, to me, you're a guy who has everything going for him. I don't mean to embarrass you, but you've got looks, personality and just about every conceivable asset that a woman looks for in a man. So, how come there's no Mrs Dunn?'

Tom smiled and replied, 'It's a question I've been asked before and I'll give the same answer to you. The lady I'd dearly like to be my Mrs Dunn is already someone else's wife and the mother of sixteen-year-old twins – and that is the honest answer to your question!'

'I guessed it had to be something like that,' said Judi. 'I even told James the solution to my question, but it's a real shame, though, because in our opinion you have so much to offer someone – it's such a waste!'

'Now you *are* embarrassing me, Judi! I'm not anyone special, it's just that I can't bring myself to accept second best and if I can't have the lady in question, then I don't want to settle for a substitute,' said Tom.

'Sure!' replied Judi. 'I do understand how you feel. It must be awful to love someone like that and to know that they belong to another. It makes me realize how lucky I am to be married to James. I knew from day one that I couldn't wish for a kinder man to spend the rest of my life with, and I fancied him like crazy!'

'Yes, I've noticed! You and James are really in tune with each other and it heightens my longing to be like that with Nicola. The truth is, Judi, it's not as if she is happily married – far from it,' replied Tom wistfully.

'Sorry, Tom,' said Judi. 'I've no right to pry into your love life, but I'm afraid that I'm a true romantic at heart and I like to know what makes people tick, so please forgive me.'

'Nothing to forgive, Judi. It's perfectly natural that you would want to know and I'm sure that if the roles were reversed, I'd be the one asking questions.'

'Look, there's James waving to us over there. He obviously wants us for a photo call, so we'd better get there,' said Judi, somewhat relieved to finish the conversation with Tom. She felt that maybe she had probed too far into what was a sensitive area of Tom's life. She felt sorry for him and only wished that she could be in a position to help.

If he had to be honest, Tom himself was pleased that the conversation had come to an end. It was one thing to think about Nicola, but a completely different ball game having to talk about her, and to hanker after a married woman didn't exactly put him in a good light.

In the afternoon the coach came to pick them up to transport them to Jasper railway station, where they would board the train for Vancouver. And what a train it proved to be! It was twenty-nine cars long and it had three engines to pull it along. They were informed that it was one quarter of a mile long with four observation domes and five dining cars. The passengers were provided with a 'cabin' each, which in day time was a comfortable place to sit and watch the world go by, but at night was transformed into a bedroom, when bunks were pulled down from the wall by the attendant.

Tom found it very difficult to sleep, with the continual swinging and swaying of the train, and in the morning his fellow passengers agreed that they had not had a peaceful night. However, what they had lacked in sleep was well compensated by what they saw at breakfast and lunch time! During the morning, Tom, James and Judi went through to one of the observation cars, to watch the fantastic scenery as the train passed by rivers, waterfalls, lakes, canyons, forests, mountains etcetera. Meantime, the train's head chef prepared them a real gourmet lunch; Tom might have been a long way from home, but this chef on the Rocky Mountain Train, sure knew how to cook!

They found the trip on the train a breathtaking experience and on reaching Vancouver station, Judi said, 'Just how lucky can we three guys get? Not only do we see these fantastic sights, but we see them all under a cloudless blue sky complete with glorious sunshine! I ask you, what more could we possibly want?'

Tom remained silent. He was tempted to say that it had all been great, but it would have been even better if he could have had the company of Nicola and shared all the sights with her. He really envied James and Judi their closeness and it made him feel that well of loneliness which was hidden deep inside his soul.

18

It was with mixed feelings that Tom placed his key into his front door latch and opened it. He felt tired after an overnight flight from Vancouver to London. It had proved to be a smooth flight, but there were always too many distractions going on in the cabin to settle down to do any serious sleeping. Also, it felt as though he had been away longer than eight days, but Tom had worked out in his mind that that was due to all the travelling he and his travelling companions had done in such a very short space of time.

Tom was very much aware that he was entering an empty house and, apart from a sleepy cat who got up half-heartedly when her master entered, it was all very, very quiet. A pile of letters had been stacked neatly on his hall table and when he went through to the kitchen there was a note in David's writing for him: *'Welcome home, Tom! Hope you had a great time in the Rockies – I'll catch up with you sometime tomorrow. Milk is in the fridge and there's some bread in the bin. Cheers! David'*.

Good old David, thought Tom. It certainly meant that he could go away from home and know that David would look after the cats and the house for him.

Tom was very conscious of the silence, having spent all last week being constantly surrounded by people, but he soon rectified that by turning on the radio, pouring himself a glass of his favourite claret and then sitting down at his study desk to open the numerous letters which he had fetched in from the hall. Tom took out a paper knife from one of the drawers and slit open the envelopes in readiness. Then he decided before perusing the letters that he would listen to any messages that were on his answerphone. He switched it on and heard the first message.

'Hi, Tom! It's Jane Shepherd. I'm not really sure which day it is you're coming back, but could we rearrange next week's appointment from Tuesday to Friday? Sorry to mess you about, but I've got to go to a funeral on Tuesday afternoon down in Kent. Hear from you soon! Bye for now – Jane.'

The second call on the machine was the very familiar voice that Tom loved so much. 'Tom, it's only me! You seem to have been away forever and yet it's only been a week! I can't say much on the answerphone. I hate the damn things anyway, but please phone me ASAP Love – Nicky!'

Tom sat back in his chair. There was something in the tone of Nicola's voice that alerted him. She was talking too quickly and yet not really telling him anything of significance that he could possibly latch on to. Nicky hadn't even given him a time that he should phone her. Surely if it was anything really important, she would have suggested a time that she would be free to speak without the presence of Graham or the twins in the house?

Tom leant forward and switched the machine back on. There were two more messages for him. One was from another of his clients and the final message was from the secretary of the health club in Walton, where he trained several of its members. Tom decided he would return all the calls tomorrow, when, hopefully, he would have had a good night's sleep back in his own bed and would wake up feeling refreshed.

His mind went back to Nicky's call. It was so unlike her to leave a message like that and what did she mean by 'phone me ASAP'? That certainly gave Tom the impression that something urgent was troubling her. There was certainly no point in returning the call right now, as, after consulting his watch, he knew that Nicola would be picking up the twins from school.

Tom really was beginning to feel extremely tired after his week's travelling and his overnight flight. It was just coming up to four o'clock and certainly some jet lag was starting to kick in. He remembered his specialist saying to him when he discharged him from the hospital, 'Now, Tom, you must listen to what your body is telling you. If you feel tired, please go and rest.'

Tom smiled to himself and decided that he would just go and have that rest now. It had been a long week and now it was time to give in to some much needed sleep. His phone messages and his pile of mail would just have to wait until tomorrow.

19

Waiting for Nicola to arrive seemed endless. They had arranged to meet for drinks and lunch at what had become their favourite restaurant in London, The Riverbridge.

After what seemed an age, Tom saw Nicola enter the lounge bar, where he had been waiting and enjoying a large glass of house red wine for the past half an hour. Nicola was looking as lovely as ever. She was dressed in a pale lilac suit which had a straight skirt and a long jacket that emphasized her beautiful slim figure. Under it she wore a very pretty white silk blouse with its collar turned out over the jacket. Her matching high-heeled shoes and clutch bag in lilac completed her outfit. Nicola's hair, which she wore at shoulder length, shone with good health and was immaculate; even her nails had been manicured and painted a very pale lilac. Tom was very conscious of the admiring glances she received from the men in the room as he walked over to greet her.

'Sorry I'm running late, Tom. I got to Waterloo station without any hitch, but my taxi got stuck in a traffic jam along the Embankment. You've not been here too long, I hope?' said Nicola, giving Tom a kiss on each cheek in greeting.

'No, darling, I've been enjoying the wait, but I must confess I was beginning to worry a little – it's so unlike you to be late. Never mind, you're here safe and sound and I'll order you a drink. What's it to be?' replied Tom, more than a little aware of his heart thumping fast at the thrill of seeing Nicola again.

He studied her closely as they sat with their drinks, looking through the menu ready to order, but her appearance gave away no clues as to what their meeting was to produce.

'Well, did you have a really good holiday last week? I thought about you a lot and wondered how you were bearing up to all the travelling after all you've been through,' said Nicola with genuine concern.

'Nicky, it was sheer magic! It was really good of James and Judi to invite me along on their trip and I enjoyed the whole experience. Can't wait to do it all over again, and next time I'd be tempted to include a cruise to Alaska, which some of our fellow travellers went on to do. The coach dropped them off at the Vancouver docks to board their ship, whilst the rest of us made our way home. But this time, I was quite happy to have just done the Rockies trip. There was just one thing missing, I have to admit, and that was you! How I'd love to have been able to share it all with you.'

'Please don't say things like that, Tom! It's like wishing for the moon or the impossible dream,' said Nicola with a deep sigh. Tom was sure he detected a tone of hopelessness in her voice.

After finishing their drinks, they went into the dining room and were shown to the table that Tom had reserved for them by the window. After having enjoyed a lovely piece of salmon, beautifully served and cooked, Tom said, 'Now come on, darling, tell me what's this lunch all about. Why the urgent message on my answer machine?'

Nicola put her knife and fork down on the plate and sat right back on her chair. She looked directly into Tom's eyes before saying, 'Tom, this last week while you've been away has been an absolute nightmare! I needed to talk to you and you were literally thousands of miles away.'

'So what's happened in the short time I've been in Canada? What was such a nightmare?' asked Tom, growing more intrigued by the minute.

'It's a long story, and I have no intention of boring you with all the details. But everything to do with my life and Graham's just came to a head. He accused me and I accused him – stalemate, really! It was a bomb exploding.'

'Hang on, darling, hang on! You're going to tell me what happened, I hope. You accused each other of what, exactly?'

'It all started on the actual evening you went away. We'd had our dinner and taken our coffee into the lounge. The twins had eaten with us and then gone up to their rooms to do their homework. I was sitting down drinking my coffee and looking at the evening paper to see if there was anything worth watching on TV, when right out of the blue, Graham said, "So is it today that lover boy has flown off to Canada?" To say that I was taken aback would be an understatement and I replied, "And what is that remark supposed to mean?" Graham went on, "You know perfectly well, Nicola, what it means! Don't give me that innocent look. You obviously think I'm completely naïve, but I can assure you here and now, I'm far from it. I have known *all* about your relationship with Tom Dunn for years. You've always been so quick to accuse me of having affairs, but I guess it's more like a case of the pot calling the kettle black!"'

'"What on earth has brought all this on, Graham?" I asked him feeling very uncomfortable by now. Then it all came out. Graham said sneeringly, "What's brought it on, as you so innocently ask, dear Nicola, is the fact that you only questioned my relationship with Kate about a fortnight ago! Kate happens to be a member of my staff and I can't help it if she rings me at home occasionally if she's got some query to raise. You are never slow to dish out accusations and yet I'm expected to sit back and let you run off to confide in Tom Dunn whenever you feel like it. Not to mention doing the Florence Nightingale bit. Oh yes, Nicola, there's definitely one law for you and another one for me!"'

20

Tom beckoned to the waiter and asked him to pour them out another cup of coffee. It was easier to talk now that they were ensconced in large comfortable chairs in the lounge bar.

'Thanks for a lovely lunch, Tom. Sorry that it's been spoilt by me going on about what happened with Graham. But I had to tell you as it will probably be the last time I'll get to see you,' said Nicola in a resigned tone of voice. 'Graham just went on and on about how there was obviously one law for me and another for him. He told me that he had known about us for a very long time and that he knew I met you in town and that he thought that I would have flung him out on his ear long ago if it wasn't for the fact that I had you to run and tell my troubles to.

'He was working himself into quite a stressful state and he went on, "If you hadn't got your precious Tom to confide in, I don't think you would have stayed with me, children or not! You're not as innocent as you like to give the impression you are! You just prefer playing the part of the wronged wife!"

'I replied that there is no harm in having a friend of the opposite sex and I thought that he would be the first to agree. "You've been out with enough women since you and I married to fill a dictionary, so what's your problem all of a sudden?" I asked him.

'Graham replied, "The problem is – correction – my problem is that I am getting really tired of having to explain everything to you, while you can just do as you damn well please! I know you feel more than friendship for Tom; you can't fool me, Nicky, so I shouldn't even try! You'll be wasting your breath."

' "So what's that meant to imply?" I asked him. I was completely on the defensive by now and wondered how he knew of my visits to see you and the fact you've been away on holiday to Canada. He seemed so very well informed.'

'So what was the outcome of the conversation, or should I say confrontation?' asked Tom, with concern for Nicola.

'Well, the long and the short of it is that Graham asked me point blank whether I wanted us to stay married, or should we go our separate ways. I didn't hesitate in replying and I said that I wanted us to stay together as a family. The twins have taken their GCSEs this year and the next two years will be spent studying for their A-levels prior to going on to university. Tom, I didn't even have to think about it! I just know that, all feelings aside, I must stay in the marriage for the sake of my children and the rest of my family.'

'I understand, darling, you don't have to explain it all to me. I know you've not been happy for a long time, but I also know where your loyalty lies, and that's with the family,' Tom said, knowing that this was what Nicola needed to hear from him. It was no use pleading with Nicola to leave and go away with him. She would never have any peace of mind knowing what she'd done.

'Graham then said that as I had decided to spend the rest of my life with him, I was to stop running to you every time something went wrong. He said that he would promise to stop seeing other women and that we must both make an effort for each other. I asked him how I would know that he was sticking to his part of the bargain and he replied that I would just have to learn to trust him. He made it all sound so simple!'

'And how do you feel about it all, Nicky? Be honest, you know that I have only ever wanted what is best for you,' asked Tom in all sincerity.

'How do you imagine I feel? I feel frightened that I've committed myself completely to Graham and I feel even more frightened that I have got to break away entirely from you! You've no idea how much it's helped knowing that you are always there for me – a shoulder to cry on. Graham was right when he said that I would have turfed him out years ago if it hadn't been for you. In a remote kind of a way, you have made me feel secure. I want to thank you for being there and I want to say sorry now for having to say goodbye to you – I never wanted to hurt you, but I can't go on like this. I've got to give my marriage another go; it's not fair the way I've been to Graham or to you. Please forgive me, Tom,' said Nicola. 'I'm not proud of the mess I've made of my life.'

'There's absolutely nothing to forgive, darling,' replied Tom. 'People come in and out of each other's lives along the way and I guess that we found a real need for each other's friendship at that particular point in time. But now, in some ways, our friendship has gone full cycle and maybe you've exhausted that need you felt for me.'

'Oh, I don't think so, Tom! I know I'll always love you and I'll always need you, but I've made a choice and I've got to stick to it, whatever's lined up for me in the future. But, please, never ever think that I've grown tired of our friendship or that I've stopped loving you,' said Nicola, and her unhappiness came out in her voice.

She got up from her chair, bent over, placed a kiss on the top of Tom's head and said, 'I've got to go now. Please don't get up and please don't follow me!' And with those words and that one brief gesture, Nicola walked out of Tom's life.

21

Tom sat in his chair, somewhat dazed. He felt that he couldn't have got up even if he'd wanted to. His mind was working overtime; so much had been said in the last three hours that it was difficult to take it all on board.

One thing was for certain, Tom didn't like the fact of Nicola walking out of his life and yet in some strange way he felt an odd sense of excitement, a kind of relief. At the end of the day, Tom had always felt that his friendship with Nicola was going absolutely nowhere and he couldn't spend the rest of his life hoping that Graham would disappear and leave the coast clear for him to step in. Life just wasn't like that. Tom had passed so much of the last twelve years just hoping and longing for something to happen so that he and Nicola would eventually be a couple, but now he had to get on with his life, without Nicola being his goal. His years of waiting in the wings had at last come to an end and Nicola, entirely herself, had taken the decision not to see him.

This last year had been peculiar for Tom in more ways than one. It had started with the tragic loss of his beloved dog, Holly. Then he was told he needed major heart surgery, closely followed by his battle with his health insurance company. Next came the actual surgery and his recovery period. Then his wonderful trip to the Canadian Rockies and now, the week after his return, the finale with Nicola. He wondered what would be next on the agenda.

Tom hoped that Graham would stick to his part of the agreement and be a proper husband to Nicola – she had so much to give and he was such an appalling taker. His energy and time should be spent making Nicola and their children happy, not gallivanting after every woman in sight.

Poor Nicola, he didn't envy her her future outlook, but he knew that she was a strong enough character to cope with what lay ahead.

As for his outlook, at least he would feel freer to make new contacts, no longer having Nicola at the forefront of his mind. Without really being conscious of it, Tom had never let anyone get too close to him, because of Nicola. Once in a while over the last few years he had met an attractive woman, but had never really pursued her, because in some bizarre way, he was 'saving himself' for Nicola. The more Tom thought about it, the more ridiculous the whole scene appeared. He also knew that he would never have been free, knowing that Nicola might eventually come to him. He could never imagine life without her and his constant longing for her, but now it had all been taken out of his hands and the future had been decided by Nicola herself.

Since his operation, he felt that he had definitely been given another chance, another shot at life. Without Nicola, he would be free to be himself and maybe, just maybe, he would be fortunate to meet the right person.

By the time Tom arrived home, he was glad to enter the stillness of his house. He actually welcomed the peace and quiet as the train journey home had been noisy and packed with rush hour travellers. Above all, his home was his sanctuary, it was where he felt both safe and secure. He went to the kitchen and made a much needed cup of coffee, and then took it into his study. The second post had arrived while he'd been up in London and a blue airmail envelope immediately caught his eye. Tom recognized Judi's handwriting on it as well as a distinct 'Vancouver' post mark. He drank his coffee whilst carefully opening the aerogramme and reading it.

16th August 1999

Hi, Tom!

We hope you're feeling fine after our week in the Rockies and that you didn't have any adverse effects from the tremendous 'roll' that we were all kept on by Steve! Wasn't it all great? James and I have really found it difficult to settle back down to the office routine – but we're getting there!

Apart from the chance to say 'Hi!' and to let you know that we're doing fine, I'm writing to say that I've given your address and phone number to the American girl – Wendy Donald – who was in our party on the coach. Do you remember the evening at Chateau Lake Louise when we shared a table with her and her mother, Enid, at dinner? We thought how nice they were and very friendly. At the end of the holiday, Wendy and I swapped telephone numbers. Vancouver is only a hundred miles up the coast to Seattle and we promised to meet up sometime to show each other the photos we'd taken en route through the Rockies.

Anyway, Wendy phoned us up last night to say that she was flying to London on the 29th of this month and staying for one night at the Cumberland Hotel. She will be en route for Scotland to visit an aunt who lives in St Andrews. The long and the short of it is that she has asked me if I thought it would be OK to contact you. I said I'm sure it would and so I've given her your telephone number, so I hope I've done the right thing and that you really won't mind!

Take care of yourself, Tom. We had such a ball on that holiday – we must repeat it again one year!

Keep me posted!

Lots of love from us,

Judi

Tom smiled to himself – Judi couldn't have chosen a better time to write to him and her letter cheered him up no end. He certainly did remember Wendy and her charming mother, and he remembered telling them about life in England. Come to think of it, he also recalled Wendy saying something about her forthcoming visit to Scotland, but it hadn't really registered with him.

Tom got up, folded the letter and put it carefully into the top drawer of his desk. He decided he would give Judi and James a call later on in the week. This evening he had a meeting to go to at the health track and he was glad he had something to take his mind off Nicola. Thinking and brooding were not for Tom – he much preferred to be where the action was. It was amazing how much Judi's letter had cheered him up, because when he had first sat down, he had felt very shell-shocked at receiving Nicola's news and her exit from his life.

22

The next few days were not easy for Tom but he was determined to cope with the sudden finality of his relationship with Nicola. Nevertheless, it had left him feeling completely desolate. It might have seemed selfish, but he had liked feeling needed by her; now he felt deprived, not only of Nicola herself, but her need for him as her trusted confidant. Tom had grown used to her phone calls and the rare meetings when she could 'escape' from Graham and the twins and just be herself for a few hours. It didn't often happen, but when it did, they had been able to enjoy visits to the theatre or dinner at The Riverbridge. How Tom loved that woman and how very difficult his life was going to be now, neither seeing nor speaking to her. However, he knew, more than anything, that he must respect her feelings and her decision, and the best way to prove how much he loved her was to allow her walk out of his life without putting up a struggle. He had made up his mind not to contact her, as it would only stir up a hornet's nest. Nicola must be left alone to get on with her life, and if he was no longer to be part of it, then so be it.

But Tom still continued to feel some sense of relief at their parting. It was as though a great burden had been lifted from him. It was a strange feeling, but there was also this other feeling of loving Nicola so much and he was finding it difficult to turn it off as you would turn a tap off. Unfortunately, life wasn't that simple and he knew that it would all take time. Time was, after all, life's greatest healer.

Tom heard the door bell ringing and went through from his study to answer it. It was David.

'Come in, David! Good to see you. I could really do with some company this evening – you must have known!'

'Hello, Tom. I hoped I'd find you at home. I didn't phone, because I'm en route to a committee meeting at the golf club and I had to drive past your front door. I just wanted to bring you a copy of *Yachting News and Views* with the "Narrow Escapes" article. Remember that evening at the Fox and Grapes when we prepared it for the magazine? You'll find it on page forty-two.'

'Thanks, I look forward to seeing it in print. Do you realize we discussed it in the pub before I had my operation and even that now seems ages ago? It makes me realize how quickly the time goes!'

'It certainly does, and, yes please, I could murder a glass of your excellent claret! They're a real bunch of stuffed shirts on the committee and I'll be glad to get the meeting over and done with,' said David, taking a glass from Tom.

'Then why do you stay on the committee if it's such a pain to you?' asked Tom. 'I'd have thought you'd have resigned years ago!'

'Well, to be honest, I like to know what's going on. I've been the club's secretary for the last ten years, so I don't think another year or two will cause me to suffer too much brain damage!'

Tom laughed. 'You're right. I should imagine that very little gets past you!'

'Talking of which, Tom, do I detect you're harbouring some kind of a problem? You seemed a bit down this evening when I arrived, and you know you're more than welcome to bend my ear.'

'Thanks for the offer, but I'm afraid that it's a problem that I can do precious little about. I've got to come to terms with it and it's something that only I can do. I'll just say, it's a matter to do with the heart – and I'm not referring to the heart that beats!'

'Ah! Then it has to be a problem to do with a lady friend! Tell me to shut up and to mind my own business, but you know I've an inquisitive mind and I'm a damn good listener, so if you want to test me out, I'm here! But, seriously, Tom, if I can help in any way at all...' said David, knowing that Tom had no intention this evening of telling him, or anyone else for that matter, but it was worth a try.

'I'll be fine, David. I just need time to sort everything out in my mind and then I can get focused again. But thanks for your offer of help, you're a good friend to have,' said Tom, and he meant it. He was going to leave it there, but continued.

'I didn't think I would have to admit this, David, but I feel I've been thrown aside – "services no longer required". I probably knew that our relationship was going nowhere, but like anyone who's ever been in love, I kept hoping. It's known as hanging on in there! Anyway, there's still life for me without Nicola and I must take heed of the song which goes "Pick yourself up, dust yourself down and start all over again!"'

David didn't envy Tom's task, but knew that his friend had the strength of character to cope.

23

This evening it felt somewhat strange to be meeting Wendy at the Cumberland Hotel and as he made his way up through the London traffic, he couldn't help wondering if he was really ready for this.

His longing for contact with Nicola proved to be as intense as ever and it was the not knowing how she was that was really beginning to get to him. Three or four times in the last few days there had been calls on his answer machine, but when he had played them back, there had been dead silence, followed by a click after a very short space of time. Tom's instinct told him that it was Nicola on the other end of the line. Maybe she had tried to reach him, but had then thought better of it and hung up.

Poor Nicola – she really did deserve so much more from life, not in a material sense, but in love and loyalty. She needed someone who could return all that she had to give, and Tom knew that he was that someone. He knew he could have made her happy and she in turn was everything he could ever want in a woman. Why on earth that wretched Graham had found her first and then treated her so appallingly, Tom would never know. He also couldn't believe that Graham had any real intention of treating her any differently in future either, despite what he'd said or promised.

Tom drove into the car park behind the hotel and found a parking space quite easily, much to his relief. He didn't mind driving up to London, but it was often the parking that proved to be the problem.

The foyer of the hotel was packed with people, in fact it reminded Tom of the concourse of a railway station rather than the entrance hall of a hotel! People were carrying suitcases, briefcases, shopping bags and there were children clinging on to their stressed parents. This hall appeared to house them all! Also, Tom was aware of a strong smell of coffee, which was wafting over from a kiosk at the far end of the foyer.

For the hundredth time, Tom wished that it was Nicola who he was about to meet up with, rather than Wendy. But he was logical enough to know that he must push all thoughts of Nicola to the back of his mind this evening.

Tom looked at his watch – it showed six thirty. He had arranged to meet Wendy in the bar outside the entrance to the carvery at a quarter to seven. So it pleased him that he was a little early for the date, as he would much rather get there first when meeting a friend of the opposite sex.

Fortunately, the bar was not the seething mass of visitors that the foyer had been and Tom noticed that there were only five tables occupied by couples enjoying their pre-dinner drinks. He walked up to the bar and ordered his glass of red wine, and took it over to a table from where he would be able to see Wendy's arrival. Actually, he couldn't really remember an awful lot about her, but he was one hundred per cent sure that he would recognize her!

It only seemed like yesterday that he had been sitting in another bar, waiting for another lady to arrive. That certain lady had travelled up from Surrey to meet him and the lady this evening had travelled over from the other side of the Atlantic. Nicola and Wendy would most probably never meet one another, but they did have something in common – they both wanted to meet Tom to share drinks and a meal with him.

After fifteen minutes, Wendy appeared on the top of the steps which led down to the bar. Tom watched her pause and look around and then he stood up and waved across to her. He saw a broad smile lighten up her face as she walked down the steps, into the bar, and over to his table. If Tom didn't know better, he would have taken Wendy for a true English rose. She had short wavy blonde hair, lovely green eyes and a peaches-and-cream complexion. Considering she was an American, her appearance was totally English. That was, until she spoke! Her American accent gave her away and she certainly had no inhibitions. She greeted Tom as if she'd known him forever, complete with a bear-like hug and a couple of kisses.

'Hi, Tom! It's really great to see you and thanks for sparing the time to spend an evening with me,' she said with enormous enthusiasm, which was completely genuine.

When Tom had finished releasing himself from her embrace, he said, 'Wendy! Welcome to England! It's lovely to see you again and I'm really glad you made contact with me. Sit down and tell me how you are and what kind of a flight you had.' Tom beckoned the barman to come and get Wendy's drinks order.

'I'm well, Tom, and my flight was good. I'm not the best of passengers when it comes to flying. I don't like the whole experience. I find that it's quite unnatural to get a huge lump of metal like that up into the sky! Anyway, I have to put up with it if I'm to visit these faraway places,' said Wendy, stopping for breath to enjoy her drink. 'More important, how have you been, Tom? Judi told me all about the major operation you had earlier on this year – what an awful ordeal for you!'

'I'm fine now, thanks. That trip to Canada couldn't have come at a better time – it was just what the doctor ordered. I really appreciated James and Judi inviting me to go along with them – it really set me up.'

'I can imagine,' said Wendy. 'They're a super couple. Judi and I got on a treat and I'm hoping we'll keep a good friendship going. I've already fixed for them to visit me in Seattle the weekend after I get back home.'

Tom found himself warming to this exceptionally nice American lady and he found her very easy to talk to. The evening passed by far too quickly. They enjoyed an excellent dinner in the hotel's carvery, when they talked about everything, and most of all, their mutual love of the great outdoors. Tom said goodbye to Wendy at around eleven thirty, first making her promise to call him if she had the time to stop off in London on her way back to the States.

'Sure, Tom. I might fly down from Scotland a day early so I can see you again. I'll phone you from my aunt's house and let you know,' said Wendy, and Tom knew that she meant it.

Although it had been an effort, Tom was pleased in the end that he had agreed to meet up with Wendy. He hadn't really felt like it, because he was still hurting so much from his loss of Nicola. But he had to admit to himself that the evening with Wendy had been fun and it had made him forget his troubles, even if it was for only one evening.

24

Three months elapsed and there had been no communication whatever from Nicola, either via the telephone or the written word. Now Tom had to admit to himself that as the weeks turned into months, it was highly unlikely that an envelope bearing Nicola's handwriting would fall from the letter box onto his hall carpet. Also, he knew by now that whenever he picked up the telephone receiver, it wouldn't be Nicola's voice ready to talk on the other end of the line.

In the beginning Tom was convinced that somehow, sometime, somewhere, Nicola would attempt to make some form of contact with him. But as the time had gone on, he knew for certain that it was only wishful thinking on his part. He knew that he would have liked to hear from her, or even about her, and he knew that he still loved her. That fact didn't even bear questioning. Tom also knew beyond a shadow of a doubt, that he would go running to her, if ever the chance arose, so deep were his feelings for her. On reflection, he was shocked at the profound effect that this woman had had on his life. He often felt sorry for people who had never fallen in love. In Tom's mind, they had missed out on that wonderful feeling of caring and loving another human being, with all its ups and downs. Nicola had made him feel alive and had got his adrenalin to work overtime.

It was now approaching Christmas and the New Year. This time it meant getting ready to celebrate the Millennium – a period of a thousand years coming to an end and another thousand years about to begin. It was little wonder that the nation was getting all hyped up! For their part Tom and David had decided to get together with a couple of friends to celebrate up in London. They had put a lot of thought into planning a night to remember. After all was said and done, it was exciting to be alive at the dawning of the next thousand years!

Tom had also been thinking about the approaching year and had already made his New Year's resolution to revisit Canada in the summer. This time, he was determined to go on to do the Alaska cruise. But this year, he had felt it would have meant too much travelling involved, so next year, God willing, he had every intention of going there. He was further encouraged by Judi, who had telephoned him earlier to say that she and James had already got the booking forms ready to fill in and was he coming along? Judi had also told him that Wendy and her mother were also thinking of doing the trip.

However, next summer was still a long way off and Tom couldn't help but wonder if he would have had any contact from Nicola by then. Something in his mind said yes, but equally, something else told him no, and he felt that it would prove the latter. As Nicola had always been fond of saying, 'Well, Tom, it's just a question of *que sera sera* – whatever will be, will be!' And he knew that saying just about said it all.

Health-wise, Tom was feeling better with each passing week and sometimes it was only the sight of his long scars when taking a shower that made him realize just how near he had come to dying or losing all of his strength. He was now, in less than a year, firing on all cylinders and the feeling was good. This morning he had been doing a fitness workout with Jane Shepherd, when suddenly she'd said, 'For goodness sake, Tom! Do you think you should be demonstrating this aerobic feat in order to keep me fit? I'm simply terrified you'll give yourself a heart attack in the process!'

Tom had replied, 'There's no way that that is going to happen, I can assure you. I'm back to physical fitness now, so for goodness sake stop worrying – I promise you I'll be fine.'

'I just think you're amazing! When I think what you've been through, and now here you are doing exercises that men half your age would be hard pushed to perform.'

'Well, remember you also fought back after major surgery, and that was no mean battle! Cancer is a terrifying disease in whichever form it appears, and so I return your compliment, I think you're pretty amazing too.'

Jane laughed and replied, 'If you ask me, I think we've got a mutual admiration society on the go!'

Tom had grown very fond of Jane and she had become a good friend of his, as well as a client. Although their lifestyles were completely different, they had one thing very much in common with one another – they had had a huge obstacle to overcome and with a lot of hard work and determination, they'd cracked it.

25

'I never did ask you how that evening went with your American friend and I've kept meaning to,' said David as he and Tom walked across the Common towards their favourite watering hole, the Fox and Grapes.

'I thought you'd taken rather longer than expected to ask me!' said Tom, smiling. 'But in answer to your question, the evening was great! Wendy is good company and we got on really well – we discussed so many different subjects. We had hoped to have another evening together before Wendy flew home, but she had to stay up in Scotland until the last minute. Her aunt had had a fall and broken her foot and so that put paid to any future plans we had.'

'So who looked after her aunt after Wendy returned to Seattle?' asked David.

'Well, Wendy arranged for her aunt to go into a nursing home for three weeks, where she knew she would be properly looked after. That took care of the immediate future, and the aunt has a lot of good friends and neighbours to keep an eye on her and visit her. Wendy flew home with peace of mind and was just thankful that she'd been there when she was most needed.'

'I should say,' replied David. 'Pity, though, that it prevented you seeing her again.'

It was a fine Saturday morning in early December and there had been a very heavy frost. But now the sun was shining from a cloudless blue sky and it felt good to be striding out across the short, crispy grass. Children were busily feeding bread to a handful of ducks on the pond; in fact, the whole scene would have made a wonderful Christmas card quite easily. Men, women and children and dogs were out on the Common in abundance, the sunshine had brought everyone out, and Tom just hoped that they wouldn't all have the same idea as David and himself and be heading for lunch at the pub!

As it turned out, he needn't have worried. The pub did have quite a few visitors already enjoying their drinks and refreshments, but, so far, it wasn't crowded. When they walked in, Tom and David even managed to get their usual table to the left of the pub's roaring fire and Tom went over to the bar to get them each a drink.

'After we've had something to eat,' said Tom, carefully putting their beers down on the table without spilling them, 'let's go for a long walk over the golf course. Once the sun goes, it will be pretty cold and we'll want to get indoors.'

'Good idea! I could certainly do with the exercise. I spend far too much of my time sitting at my desk at the office in the week, and I know that a long, brisk walk will do me a power of good,' replied David.

Their food arrived – sausages and mash with onion gravy, which was one of the pub's special dishes and Tom and David's favourite. After finishing their food and enjoying a cup of coffee, Tom said, 'I've got a bit of news for you, David. As we got on to the subject of Wendy earlier, how about her joining us for the Millennium celebrations?'

'Sounds like good news to me! How's that come about when she lives miles away in the States?'

'She's coming over to Scotland again to visit her aunt, but this time she's with her parents. Originally, they invited the aunt over to them, but after her fall, they thought it best if they came over here. Wendy called me to say she was coming with her parents, but could she join me to celebrate the Millennium? I said, "You bet you can!" It's really given me a lift, and to be honest, I can't wait to see her again,' said Tom with a twinkle in his eye and a smile stretching from ear to ear.

'I do believe you're smitten, Tom! I ask myself, are you looking pleased, or are you looking pleased?' said David, who had been well aware of the awful year his friend had had to put up with. David had really admired Tom for the way in which he had got on with his life, despite all the recent traumas he'd had. Outwardly, Tom always appeared cool, calm and collected, but he couldn't fool David, because he knew his friend extremely well.

'You could say that!' replied Tom. 'I have to be honest, I was really disappointed when she phoned me to say she had to fly straight home instead of breaking the journey in London.'

'So how come she gets to spend the Millennium with us?' asked David. 'Won't she be doing her celebrating up in Scotland with her parents and her aunt?'

'Obviously not,' replied Tom. 'She's made it abundantly clear that she would like to celebrate with me.'

'Terrific! That means I get to meet your lady from across the Atlantic. Roll on the Millennium! Anyway, you have hardly told me anything about Wendy – how old is she, what does she do, has she been married or what?' asked David, who was more than a little intrigued by Tom's friend from Seattle.

'Hold on, David! What is this – an inquisition? But to answer your question, has she been married or what? No, she's never been married, but she did live with someone for five years when she was working in Boston on a women's magazine as the features editor. They got engaged, but the guy couldn't cope with the marriage bit and so they split up and went their separate ways. Wendy was really devastated and, within a couple of months, she resigned from her job, sold the apartment and moved back to Seattle. She's been living with her parents for the past four years and works at a secretarial college in Seattle teaching journalism, which she loves. She's thirty-seven, and so she's still a little way off the big four O, and that makes her ten years my junior,' said Tom, who had grown used to David's interest in his lady friends' credentials over the years. But it was good to have a friend who cared and could be trusted. David had been widowed several years ago, when his wife,

Jackie, had been tragically killed in a car accident. He had been left to bring up his young son Richard, but had never wanted to marry again.

26

Christmas arrived, and with it the first communication from Nicola. It came in the form of a Christmas card and, in many ways, Tom wished she hadn't bothered. The card was very formal, bearing the printed greeting *Wishing you a very Happy Christmas and a wonderful Millennium – from Graham, Nicola, Sophie and Andrew.* There was no message added to the printed words and not even so much as a 'Hi' to him from Nicola. Tom had felt an immediate surge of emptiness in the pit of his stomach as he had added their card to the rest he'd already received. It wouldn't have hurt Nicola to have added just a sentence to let Tom know that all was well with her.

It had now been four months since they had shared their final lunch together at The Riverbridge and Nicola had told Tom of her decision to sever all contact with him. It may have seemed a petty reaction, but Tom sent a card to the four of them and simply signed it *Tom* – he reckoned that what was good for the goose, was good for the gander!

To pretend that he didn't still think about Nicola on a daily basis would be to lie. He did think about her, but the hurt had eased somewhat with the passing of time. Tom knew that it would and he also knew that his growing friendship and interest in Wendy was all contributing to this state of affairs. Tom thought about Wendy a great deal and he couldn't wait for the Millennium celebrations to start, when he would be able to enjoy her company once again.

Following Wendy's visit, she and Tom had regularly e-mailed each other and she had also sent over a set of photographs which she had taken of the holiday in the

Rockies. There was one photo in particular that he had liked, the one with them all in it, taken along the water's edge at Lake Louise. The photo showed a smiling and happy Wendy, her mother, James, Judi and himself. He remembered it being taken by Todd, their tour guide, as they had walked for a while after breakfast and before Todd got them to board the coach once more. Tom had got a frame and had put the photo in it and then placed it on his desk in the study. It was a wonderful reminder of his Canadian holiday and it had captured their delight at being at Chateau Lake Louise on film.

Tom wondered how he would react if Nicola were to call him now. Not very well, he thought. The end of their relationship had come right of the blue and Nicola had done it so abruptly. He hadn't expected to meet up with her again, but he had more than half expected to receive at least a telephone call from her, or perhaps a letter, and now, four months on, he'd received this formal, cold Christmas card. Nicola had spent so many years telling Tom how much she needed him to be there for her. Now, the year when he'd had to have major heart surgery, she'd dropped him like a discarded glove and it had hurt. He still felt deprived of a very special friend. Nicola had definitely left a gap in his life, despite the fact that he was always busy, professionally and socially.

Christmas arrived and Tom went to stay in Eastbourne with his sister, Vicky, and her husband, Bill. Tom's parents had died ten years ago. His father had died of a massive heart attack and his mother had died of one also. It had been a terrible year for Tom and Vicky to contend with, visiting their mother in hospital and later watching her slowly die in the hospice. Six months after their mother's death, their father died. There had been no warning signs, he had simply been sitting on the end of his bed putting his shoes on. He had leant over to tie the shoe laces and fallen off the bed like a stone. It was a sudden death at the age of sixty-one and it had left Tom and Vicky shocked and extremely upset. Tom remembered how he had turned to

Nicola in his hour of need and she had comforted him with her kindness.

Vicky and Bill ran a very successful marketing and public relations firm in the heart of Eastbourne. They had a modern well-equipped office and a great team on their staff. Their home was situated a couple of miles away on the outskirts of the town and Tom enjoyed his visits to them, not only at Christmas, but at various other times throughout the year. Christmas in Eastbourne had become a tradition and Tom looked forward to it each year.

Two days after Boxing Day, Tom drove back to his home in Wimbledon – and the countdown to the Millennium began. David had booked a couple of nights in London at a little hotel on the south of Soho Square. It had been the private house of a political essayist before it was converted into a hotel. After lengthy discussions with Tom, David thought it would be a perfect venue to take an American to. 'It has so much going for it, Tom! It's very English, very elegant and very old-fashioned. You know how the Americans love that sort of thing. And the building has lots of history attached to it. Also, we'll be up there in the heart of London ready for the big night. We can travel up to town by train, book in at our hotel and take it from there!'

'So how many of us have you booked for, to go on this New Year spree?' asked Tom, who had left all the arrangements in David's capable hands.

'Six,' replied David. 'There will be you, me, Richard and his fiancée, Sarah, Caroline, my friend from the office, who has eagerly agreed to share a four-poster bed with me – no questions from you, please, Tom! You've met Caroline lots of times and I shall say no more at this stage.'

'You're a dark horse, David! But good luck to you – I always thought that Caroline had a thing about you and I guess I was right.'

'Absolutely no comment!' said David, grinning away like a Cheshire cat. 'And, of course, the sixth member of our party, is your American friend Wendy.'

27

Tom stood on the concourse of the airport waiting to meet Wendy and her parents off the flight coming into Heathrow from Seattle. It was the morning of 30th December. Later in the day, Wendy would be travelling up with Tom to London, where they would join Tom's friends in readiness for the Millennium celebrations. Wendy's parents, Enid and Geoff, would be heading up to Scotland to do their celebrating with Enid's sister, Kate.

Tom's feelings on this particular December morning were a mixture of excitement tinged with anticipation. If the truth were really known, he'd admit that he couldn't wait to see Wendy again. He had been at the airport for well over an hour, as the last thing he had needed was to be late in meeting them. Their plane was due to land at eleven thirty and he had been over to find out exactly where they would arrive, after they had cleared customs. He had also checked that their plane was due in on time, which, thankfully, it was.

While he still had a little time to spare, he decided to get himself a cup of coffee and a copy of the *Daily Mail*, and watch the world go by. It was amazing to observe all the people of different nationalities, dashing about from pillar to post – everywhere at the airport was an absolute buzz. The image of things to come, thought Tom to himself, as he imagined what it would be like up in London for the Millennium.

When Tom had finished drinking an excellent cup of cappuccino, he made his way over to the arrivals area. He wondered what Wendy's father, Geoff, would be like. Tom remembered her mother from the Canadian holiday as a quiet, gentle lady. He had remarked to Wendy how quiet her mother was for an American. Usually, they were very outgoing and outspoken, full of confidence, but Enid didn't appear like that at all.

'Well, you see, Tom, my mom met my father when they were both studying for a business degree at Yale University. They fell in love, got married and my mom settled in America. She originally comes from Scotland and I think she missed it a great deal to begin with, but she was really in love with my father and so she chose to live where he was based and was happy just to be with him. So that makes me half American and half Scottish,' said Wendy with pride.

In no time at all the passengers off the Seattle flight began filtering through the arrivals entrance. Tom looked around anxiously for the first sight of Wendy and her parents. He didn't have long to wait, for there, wearing a cerise trouser suit and looking as bright as a button, was Wendy, who was busy waving and smiling across to him. Tom swore that his heart missed a beat as she came running over towards him. When she reached him, she put her shoulder bag and holdall down and hurled herself into his open arms. She seemed quite oblivious to the fact that her parents were right behind her, her father pushing their heavily laden luggage trolley.

'Oh, Tom, it's great to see you! I hoped you'd be here on time to meet us and I can't tell you how much I've been looking forward to this visit!' said Wendy, and after she had finished embracing Tom, she turned round to where her parents were waiting. 'Tom, meet my father, Geoff. You already know my mom, Enid.'

Tom laughed at Wendy's obvious excitement at being with him again and then shook hands with Geoff, next giving Enid a kiss on both cheeks, before saying, 'It's good to meet you, Geoff, and to see you again, Enid. Welcome to Britain! First things first, let's get your luggage sorted and we'll get it over to Terminal One and check it in for your afternoon flight for Aberdeen. Wendy tells me that you will have a hire car waiting for you at the airport, so you can drive directly to St Andrews. Incidently, I've already confirmed your departure time for three o'clock.'

'Well done, Tom! I like an efficient guy around and it sure will be a relief to get rid of these darned suitcases. Then perhaps you can point us in the right direction for some food. I'm starving – airline food never seems like proper food to me!' exclaimed Geoff.

Tom warmed immediately to Geoff and thought how lucky Wendy was to have such an extremely nice father. Tom saw that she had inherited her father's looks, his blond hair and green eyes. Enid's hair was nearly grey, but she'd obviously had highlights added, so it gave the overall impression of still being pretty fair. Tom guessed that in her younger days she would have been a very pretty lady, and even now she was still attractive, with a flawless skin and a lovely slim figure, despite the advancing years.

It didn't take long for them to walk over to Terminal One to get Enid and Geoff's suitcases checked in. Tom then found them a suitable café to have some lunch and made quite sure that Geoff's hunger pangs were well and truly satisfied.

Tom discovered that Wendy's parents were every bit as easy to get along with as she was. They all talked nineteen to the dozen throughout their lunch and Tom very quickly sensed the rapport that was forming between them. He felt as though he had always known this charming family from the States.

28

Driving up to London with Wendy after having seen Enid and Geoff safely off on their flight up to Scotland, Tom said, 'Now, Wendy, I suggest that you have a good rest when we get to the hotel and, on second thoughts, I insist that you do! The jet lag is bound to kick in sooner or later, so you've got to give in to it. David and the others won't be arriving until eightish and that gives you a couple of hours at least.'

'And how do you know that I even suffer from jet lag?' asked Wendy, turning round in the passenger seat so she could look at Tom while she answered him.

Tom was busy concentrating on the ever increasing traffic as he got nearer in to London. 'Well, let's put it this way! I assume, like the rest of us mere mortals, that you will get jet lag after a twelve-hour flight,' said Tom, glancing for a second at Wendy and giving her a smile.

'Absolutely right, but I don't want to waste a second of my precious time in London. I'll have a rest if you promise to wake me when your friends arrive and they're waiting to go out to paint the town.'

'We're not exactly going to, as you put it, paint the town, this evening, darling! We're going to ease ourselves gently into the London scene, bit by bit.'

Wendy laughed. She was feeling so relaxed in Tom's presence, it was as if she had known him all her life. 'OK, Tom, I'll do as I'm told, I promise.'

Tom found the car park near the hotel that David had told him about and parked his car. David and the others were making their way up by train, after they had finished working. Tom had decided that it would be best for him to drive straight from the airport, rather than go back to his home in Wimbledon first. Also, it would give more time for Wendy to have a rest, before the socializing got under way.

The hotel in Soho Square was just as David had described it and Tom was duly impressed. He carried his case and Wendy's into the foyer and walked over to the reception desk to register and collect the keys to their rooms.

'Welcome, Mr Dunn and Miss Donald! I trust you will enjoy your stay with us,' said a beautifully spoken receptionist. Tom thought how well she blended into the set-up of such an elegant hotel. 'If you will follow the porter, he will take your cases up to your rooms. You and Miss Donald have been allocated rooms 216 and 217, which are next to each other on the second floor. The rest of your party are also on the same floor. If there's anything you need, just phone reception to let us know.'

'Thank you,' replied Tom, and having duly signed the visitors' book, followed the porter with their cases to the lift.

Once in his room, Tom started to unpack. He noticed a tray bearing a kettle, teapot, cups and saucers, milk and sugar, coffee bags and tea bags, and decided to make some coffee whilst in the process of unpacking and then take a cup through to Wendy next door.

He knocked on her door and she opened it within seconds. She looked at Tom complete with coffee and said, 'Tom, great minds think alike! I've just made myself a cup of coffee, so come on in, and you can drink the one you've made.'

Tom went into her room and sat down on one of the two armchairs which were placed either side of a table by the window. 'I hope you like your room, Wendy. I can always change it if you don't.'

'It's great, Tom, thanks! It's really full of character and I just love the chintz bedspread with the matching curtains. Look at the wash stand, complete with a porcelain bowl on it. Isn't it quaint? It's a far cry from the modern wash basins I've been used to seeing,' said Wendy in her familiar American drawl which Tom found so appealing.

'It's just gone five o'clock, Wendy, so you can give in to that time clock of yours. I'll ring you through at seven thirty to wake you up. Then it will nearly be time to meet the others. When we're all present and correct, we can go out for a light supper,' said Tom, draining the last of his coffee and standing up ready to leave Wendy in peace.

'Yes, sir!' replied Wendy. 'Whatever you say, sir! But it's a good idea and I'll do as I'm told and take a rest now – the travelling and excitement are starting to catch up. If I get a couple of hours' shut-eye, I'll be all bright eyed and bushy-tailed when David and the others arrive. I'm sure looking forward to meeting them!'

Three hours on and introductions complete, the six of them headed out of the hotel and onto the streets of London. Wendy, having had her rest, linked her arm through Tom's as they walked along as if it was the most natural gesture, and Tom liked the feeling.

It had been a long day for them all, especially for Wendy, and they had agreed that some wine and a light meal was what was needed. They walked around Chinatown for a while, looking at the different restaurants and reading the menus, which were more often than not strategically placed by the doorways. It didn't take them long to find a suitable one. The meal proved to be good wholesome Chinese food, accompanied by a couple of bottles of Mateus Rosé wine, which Tom always maintained went perfectly with a Chinese meal. The round table gave Wendy the opportunity to get to know David and Caroline, and Richard and Sarah. She even found that she and Caroline had some mutual acquaintances from their work in the magazine world. Tom was thrilled to see how well Wendy fitted in with David and the others, and he was perhaps even a little jealous at the ease with which she discussed the latest pop stars with Sarah, who was only twenty.

After supper they headed back to their hotel. Goodnights were said on the landing of the second floor, before they made their way to their respective bedrooms.

   Tom lay awake for ages thinking about the day's events. He was so glad that Wendy was here with him to celebrate the Millennium and he was already looking forward to seeing her in the morning. He realized that he had not given a thought to Nicola throughout the time he'd been with Wendy until now, and it was already fast approaching midnight. He tried to imagine what their supper would have been like if it had been at The Riverbridge with Nicola, but he found it was not as easy as it once was to imagine Nicola being part of his activities. He couldn't help wondering, though, how and where she planned to celebrate the Millennium and with whom, but it certainly didn't worry him. He was still not absolutely certain how he really felt about Nicola now, but he was quite content to know that Wendy was safely tucked up in bed in the next room and that she was there only because she wanted to be with him.

29

New Year's Eve dawned fine and dry, but with a cold chill in the air. Tom and his friends met in the dining room at eight thirty, as had been arranged the evening before.

'I do love your English breakfast!' exclaimed Wendy. She had appeared today dressed in an emerald green trouser suit and had on a pair of trainers ready to tackle their day's walkabout in London. Tom thought how well she looked and how well-dressed. The colour she had chosen for today emphasized the green of her eyes and he had an overwhelming desire to get up from his chair and go over to kiss her, but thought better of it in the middle of their breakfast – somehow, he didn't think she'd appreciate it right now!

David and Caroline seemed to be getting along really well and Tom noticed that Caroline hung on David's every word. They had arrived in the dining room holding hands, so Tom guessed they'd spent a good night together in the four-poster!

Richard, David's son, was with Sarah. After having gone out together for a couple of years, they had announced their engagement on Christmas Day. David had been really pleased for them. 'Great news! You'll be able to get married in the year 2000 – and that's certainly something to mark the Millennium! Well done, both of you!' David had always been very close to Richard, his only child, and more so following the death of his young wife, which had come as such a blow to him. He had become both mother and father to Richard. Tom still wondered, all these years later, if David had ever really got over Jackie's death.

Breakfast completed, they arranged to meet in the hotel

foyer at ten o'clock and then they would set off for their day's sightseeing.

Their first port of call was an Italian restaurant they'd seen in Soho the previous night. They'd all agreed then that it looked a likely venue for their dinner the next evening and now Tom walked over to the maitre d' and said, 'Can we book a table for six people tonight?'

'I'm afraid we're not taking bookings, sir, but if you can be here by seven thirty, I'll make sure you get a table.'

'Fine! We'll aim to be here shortly after seven. We're looking forward to it,' replied Tom.

As they walked away from the restaurant, Wendy once again quite naturally put her arm through Tom's and they set off down to Trafalgar Square, pausing for a while to look at the massive Christmas tree that Norway sends over each year as a gift to Britain.

'I bet that the hundreds of pigeons in the square think it's been sent over for their benefit alone! Look at them all sitting up in the branches,' said Tom, pointing out the birds to them.

They walked through Admiralty Arch and along the Mall towards Buckingham Palace. The Queen had given her special permission this year for a funfair to be erected in the Mall and they wandered about looking at everything on display there. The six of them all went on the helter-skelter. Wendy admitted that she was a little apprehensive, as it was her first time on one, but once she'd come down it, she was all for doing it a second time! They made their way down to Buckingham Palace and then across to Westminster Bridge, where they watched a team flying their kites. The kites made very colourful and intricate patterns in the clear skies above the river.

Afterwards, at a late lunch in a little café not far from the bridge, where they had enjoyed jacket potatoes with various fillings, Wendy exclaimed, 'We've walked a long way and I think we deserved our potatoes! We've seen such a lot this morning and I can feel the atmosphere really building up – I guess it will be amazing by the time the evening gets here.'

'Absolutely right, darling,' replied Tom. 'It's going to be quite something and I think we've chosen the right place to experience it all.'

After lunch they headed back to the hotel, reaching it in plenty of time to rest and prepare for the evening. They'd already agreed to spend a couple of leisurely hours relaxing, reading their newspapers etc., so as to be refreshed for their long night out, which would start with their meal at the Italian restaurant.

'I intend to make myself a cup of coffee and then lie on my bed to watch a little of your English TV, and then I'll shower and change in readiness for our revelry. I can't wait for the fun to start!' said Wendy in the lift on the way up to their rooms.

'Good for you, Wendy and I'm certain you won't be disappointed. We're going to have a good time,' said David, who had taken an instant liking to this bubbly American friend of Tom's. In his opinion, Wendy was proving to be just what Tom needed. He knew his friend's feeling had gone deep for Nicola and he also knew how much she had hurt him. It was David's personal belief that the way in which she had ended their friendship had been so abrupt and unnecessary. Now, having spent last evening and most of today in Tom and Wendy's company, David could sense something was growing between them, and it was something good. It wasn't just the atmosphere of the Millennium approaching, it was a feeling of need and love between two human beings.

30

As promised earlier, the table in the Italian restaurant was waiting for them and they were greeted with a glass of champagne each. 'On the house!' the manager exclaimed. 'And a very happy New Year to you all!'

The restaurant was decorated with the banners for the Millennium and there were coloured balloons everywhere. The Italian waiters were dressed up in party hats and were in a real fun mode, flirting with all the lady guests and thoroughly entering into the party scene.

'Great, we've chosen well!' exclaimed David. 'When we saw the place this morning, it was just a very nice-looking Italian restaurant, but tonight it's come alive and there's a real buzz.' They all agreed with him and stayed eating and drinking until about eleven o'clock.

'Look at the long queue that's formed outside! All those people trying to get a table. If we'd have left it any later, we'd never have got in, we'd be in that crush,' said Caroline.

'Well, the saying goes, "The early bird catches the worm", and I guess we did just that!' replied David as they stood at the reception desk to settle their bill. 'Look, already another six people are sitting at our table.'

Once outside, they walked through Chinatown, down Charing Cross Road and via Trafalgar Square to the Strand. They were going to try to make their way, as thousands of other people were trying to do, down to the River Thames to see the New Year in. Everyone around them was in a very happy mood and the atmosphere had really revved up while they had been in the restaurant. There were crowds of people everywhere – it was amazing where they had all come from.

'There's thousands of people with the same idea as us,' said Tom. 'For goodness sake, make sure that we all keep together. We don't want to get separated in the crowds.' Tom could feel Wendy moving even closer to him and he instinctively put his arm around her shoulders and kissed her cheek.

'What was that for?' she asked, and laughed.

'Because I wanted to!' replied Tom. He suddenly felt very protective towards her. After all was said and done, she'd come a hell of a long way to spend this very special New Year's Eve with him; Tom could sense how much she wanted to be with him and it made him feel good.

They tried making their way down a narrow street via The Coal Hole pub near the Embankment, but found that it was blocked off by the police. Next they tried to cross Waterloo Bridge, but were stopped once again. The police weren't letting any more people onto the bridge for safety reasons. So Tom and his party continued walking, past the Law Courts towards St Paul's Cathedral.

Wendy remarked, 'Oh look, you guys, doesn't the cathedral look wonderful all lit up – wow!'

Once again they tried to get down to the river, but the closest they could get, was to stand on the Queen Elizabeth Embankment, and that still meant that they were about a hundred yards away from the actual river. But they settled for that – they were near enough.

Their hotel had generously given them each a half bottle of champagne to enjoy at midnight and they produced them out of their pockets to open as the clocks struck up and the Millennium arrived.

'Listen to all the bells of the local churches pealing out in the City!' exclaimed Tom excitedly. 'We can hear half a dozen at least and that includes St Paul's!'

They all drank their champagne from the bottles and toasted each other. Everywhere was magic, everyone was hugging and kissing and there was the singing of 'Auld Lang Syne' coming from every direction possible.

'I wouldn't have missed this for the world, Tom,' said Wendy. 'I'm already in love with London!'

Tom replied, 'I know exactly how you are feeling, and thank you for being here for me to wish you a very, very happy New Year and a happy Millennium!' With those words, Tom took Wendy into his arms and held her close. He kissed her long and hard on the lips and, for a few precious moments, they were oblivious to everyone and everything around them.

Tom became aware of David and Caroline standing close and watching them. They were both smiling. 'When you two have time to come up for air, just look at all the fireworks being let off by the passing barges. They're lighting up the whole scene from Tower Bridge to Westminster,' said David, pointing to the brilliance of it all.

At least fourteen or fifteen barges sailed past. Each barge was letting off bigger and louder fireworks than the previous one and after a quarter of an hour or so they ended in a crescendo of light, colour and noise.

By now it was getting cold and David suggested that they should make their way back to the hotel. They didn't take much persuading and agreed readily to begin their trek.

To greet them there was more champagne! The hotel manager and staff were in the foyer to welcome their guests as they arrived back. There was a glass of champagne and smoked salmon sandwiches – totally unexpected at two o'clock in the morning of the Millennium, but, nevertheless, a wonderful ending to their celebrations.

When Tom eventually got into bed, his body felt weary but his thoughts were still racing. Thoughts that were dominated by Wendy! He remembered the way they had held each other and kissed and how good it had felt; how he hadn't wanted to say good night and go off to their separate rooms. But Tom knew better than to rush things, their relationship must be allowed to grow. They had both been hurt in the past and now anything in the future must be taken one step at a time. It would have been all too easy to have invited Wendy into his room in these early hours of the year 2000 and he was pretty certain that she wanted him to, but he had held back, the passion must wait. Tom knew he was falling in love with Wendy, but he still hadn't completely got over the loss of Nicola, and part of him was still confused. And Wendy, too, could be on the rebound. They had come a long way in such a short time and, although Tom knew that he wanted her, he also wanted to make sure that this time he got it right.

31

'As dearly as I love my parents and my aunt, I don't feel a bit like going to join them in Scotland. I'd much rather be staying on in London with you, Tom,' said Wendy on New Year's Day as they sat in the lounge, enjoying a cup of coffee, waiting for the porter to bring their cases down from their rooms. The others were still finishing doing their packing.

'Well, darling,' replied Tom, 'I'm not going to be in London. After I've driven you to the airport and seen you off, I'm going straight home to Wimbledon. I want to get unpacked and installed, ready to begin work tomorrow. Would you believe, I've already got six clients lined up? They seem really keen to get back to their exercises after the Christmas and New Year break, even though tomorrow is Sunday.'

'You can't blame them. They'll be needing to exercise and possibly lose some weight, after the long binge. I count myself one of the lucky ones – I can eat and drink whatever I want to without piling the extra pounds on.'

'True! But you know that exercise is the real answer if you want to keep the weight off and keep fit,' replied Tom.

'You should know!' replied Wendy, smiling across at Tom. 'Here speaketh our fitness trainer. But it still doesn't make me want to go up to Scotland, even if you do have to work a few people out! I've had the most fantastic forty-eight hours, meeting your friends, celebrating with them and then enjoying getting to know some of London by day and night. I can't begin to tell you how much I've enjoyed myself,' said Wendy, and meant every word.

'All good things come to an end, darling,' said Tom, who

was not looking forward to Wendy's departure any more than she was.

'But this time, it's not an end, it's a new beginning. The beginning of a new century – you can't talk about an end at this stage.'

'No, I meant it's come to the end of our celebrations with David and the others, and now it's back to reality. You'll probably have a great five days in Scotland before you fly home. Your parents and your aunt will really be looking forward to your company.'

'I guess you're right, but it still doesn't make going any the easier and I don't relish having to say goodbye to you and your friends. It's been magic being here with you all,' said Wendy. 'Tom, will you come and visit me in Seattle? You'd be more than welcome and I'd love showing you around my stomping ground! How about it? Do you fancy coming? Maybe sometime in February – that's not too far away.'

'I'd love to visit you, darling, but February is no good as far as I'm concerned. I've already accepted an invitation to join a ski party from the International School of Düsseldorf to go to Crans Montana in Switzerland.'

'Are you really ready to ski again, Tom?' asked Wendy with genuine concern. 'Are you fit enough?'

'I'm sure I am,' came Tom's quick reply. 'I've been going on this trip for the last fifteen years. The trip leaders are my old friends Martin and Cass Muller. I've known them for twenty-five years – we met as students, skiing. Now we take a group of about sixty teenage students, mainly Americans, plus some Japanese. I run the ski classes.'

'It sounds good to me, Tom. I know how much you love to ski. You first told me that when we were in Chateau Lake Louise and surrounded by all those wonderful mountains! But do you get enough back-up with it all – it sounds like a hell of a lot of students to me!'

'We usually hire six teachers from the local ski school and we try to use the same ones each year. We also have two qualified teachers from the Düsseldorf School, so I'm provided with ample practical support. You mustn't worry about me, Wendy, skiing is second nature to me,' said Tom, who could sense Wendy's concern, but was inwardly flattered that she did care about his well being.

'If you say so, Tom. I still reckon that it's way too early for you to take to the slopes. I've also heard that Crans Montana is a very chic Swiss resort – very expensive and exclusive, just teeming with rich people. So I'm a little a bit jealous that I can't come.'

'You are absolutely right about the resort, darling,' replied Tom. 'It's also a very beautiful place with south-facing slopes which catch the sun on most days.'

'So you've really made your mind up – you intend to go?' asked Wendy, wishing all the while that Tom would have the sense to put off his skiing for a little longer.

'Yes, I really have made up my mind and I intend to go! You'll just have to trust me to arrive home in one piece, but far fitter from the experience,' said Tom with a huge grin on his face.

'So when are you going to visit us in Seattle?' asked Wendy, who guessed it was better not to pursue the planned ski trip any further.

'Probably Easter would be a good time. I usually take a few days' break then as several clients are away for the Easter holiday. How would that be for you and your parents?'

'I guess that would be fine with us. It's great for me as I'm on holiday from college and I'm sure it would be OK as far as my mom and dad are concerned. It will sure make saying goodbye a whole heap easier if I've got your visit sorted,' said Wendy, and then, to Tom's surprise, she started to cry.

'Don't, Wendy, please don't! I promise I'll come to Seattle at Easter and we'll have a ball. It will be something for us both to look forward to and, in the meantime, we'll keep in close contact e-mailing and phoning. Everything is going to be all right; as you said yourself, this is the beginning, not the end!'

Tom knew Wendy well enough now to know that her tears were very genuine and he went over to comfort her as best he could.

32

The first four days of Tom's ski trip to Crans Montana were uneventful. The party of students were well-behaved, very keen and very good. Each day they had enjoyed skiing under clear blue skies with unbroken sunshine, it proved to be perfect weather for skiing.

On day five, Tom and his party headed for Plaine Morte. It was the top of one of the furthest mountains, so called because nothing lived up there. It was just one big glacier, three thousand metres above sea level.

Tom noticed that the wind had started to pick up and one or two clouds had formed, but it was nothing untoward. His group managed to reach the top successfully and were beginning to ski down, when Tom suddenly realized that a storm was brewing up pretty quickly. However, he had the top group of skiers with him and so he was not unduly worried. He instructed them to get their anoraks, hats and snow goggles out of their backpacks. This was a complete contrast to the clothing they had been wearing for the last four days, when they had worn T-shirts in the warmth of the sun.

'Tom, I haven't got any of my warm clothes with me, I left them in the hotel,' said Naomi, who was one of the weakest skiers in his group.

Oh you stupid girl, thought Tom, but in the circumstances he just said, 'What a silly thing to do.' He had a spare hat, which he handed her, while someone else was able to give her a thick pair of gloves and someone else had a spare pair of goggles which she could use.

With that sorted out, Tom said, 'Now let's get a move on and get down to the lift, so that we can get to safety and have some lunch!'

But within ten minutes the storm broke, bringing with it thick cloud, heavy snowflakes and virtually no visibility. Tom had already discounted skiing all the way back to the village, which would have taken them between thirty and forty minutes. He was also concerned that by now Naomi was freezing, and would she last that amount of time? Tom had therefore decided that the best option was to go across by lift to the other mountain, where the restaurant was, and Naomi could get warmer very much sooner. On a good day, this lift ride would normally take ten minutes.

They got to the bottom of the lift and then Tom had another decision to make – should they take the drag or the chair lift? Tom guessed that the chair would be too cold and might suddenly stop, so he chose the drag. He sent the students up first and then followed them up. Within fifty metres, Tom saw that Emilio – disorientated by the falling snow – had fallen off the drag lift. He was one of the better skiers so Tom yelled at him through the wind, 'Emilio! Go back to the bottom of the lift and start again. We'll meet you at the top!'

Three hundred metres later, Tom saw another faller – it was Yuko, who was the youngest in his group. However, by this time, they were above some treacherous outcrops of rock, which even in good weather proved tricky, but could be fateful in these awful conditions. So although Yuko was a very good skier Tom screamed at her, 'Traverse across for four or five hundred metres before you go down to the lift start!' Tom knew that that was where she would find the prepared piste and would be able to ski down to get the lift up to rejoin their group.

Tom's nightmare continued, as less than fifty metres later he saw Mike – a big strong basketball player – fall off the drag. Tom yelled the same instructions over to Mike: 'Traverse across for four or five hundred metres before you go down to the lift start!' and then Tom was faced with yet another decision. Should he get off the drag to help the fallen skiers or should he stay on? But as there could be more fallers, he decided to stay put. Fortunately, there weren't.

When they reached the lift top, Naomi was looking extremely cold; a T-shirt provided no protection at all in these freezing conditions. Tom wondered whether he should give his anorak to her, but knew that he had to stay warm and alert if he was to lead the party to safety. They waited by the lift for the others, but after five minutes they had to make a move because Naomi was getting very cold. The others tried to shelter her with their bodies, but it was difficult with their skis on.

By this time Emilio had arrived at the top of the lift. He gave his apologies for falling off, but Tom had no time to discuss it with him there and then. His concern was whether he should wait for the others or set off to look for them. He could see Naomi getting bluer and bluer and Tom knew that he would have to keep her on the move. So he decided to go to look for Yuko and Mike.

Tom didn't really want to do this, as it was the steepest black slope in the resort. It was even tough in good visibility, let alone in these conditions. He also had to keep his party with him, and moving. Despite all this, Tom started off and slowly led them down. Cautiously, he stopped at each ridge, so he could test with his ski stick whether there was snow, rock or air on the other side.

33

It took an age to get to the bottom and they saw no sign of the lost skiers. There was nothing left to do but to head up on the lift once again. Tom said to them, 'Right! I don't want any fallers this time around – just hold on tight!'

They all safely reached the top, but Naomi was getting really weak by this time. Tom led them across to the final short lift, which would take them up to the restaurant. Everyone got on and Tom made sure that Naomi was just in front of him, so that he could watch her. Every few seconds, he could see how she was lurching to the left or to the right and he screamed over to her, 'Stay upright, Naomi. Keep the legs wide!' Miraculously, she managed to do just that. They arrived at the top and Tom sent everyone down a short hundred-metre piste, which fortunately they all knew well, to safety.

In the meantime, Tom got Naomi to put her skis behind his and they snow-ploughed down to the bottom. There they kicked their skis off and Tom wrapped her in his anorak and carried her inside. He was more than a little relieved to see his friend Cass, who had been alerted to the situation by the others, and he thankfully handed Naomi over into her care.

With Naomi being looked after, Tom's next concern was to go out once more into the appalling weather to find Yuko and Mike. He grabbed Martin and one of the other instructors and headed off in search of them. It wasn't easy but eventually they found them sheltered beneath some rocks, just off the piste, two hundred metres from the bottom of the first lift. They had both become disorientated and had lost their bearings. They hadn't wanted to ski over the edge of the cliff, so had decided that their best plan was to stay put. Tom led them back to the lift and then on to the safety of the restaurant, much to everyone's relief, but especially Tom's!

Reflecting later on the whole episode, Tom wondered several things. Should he have checked their equipment, before they had left the hotel? Were they too high? Did he miss a weather report? Should he have got off the first lift? Should he have lent Naomi his anorak? The questions were going round and round in his mind.

Back in the warmth of the hotel in Crans Montana, Tom discussed it over for hours with the 'men of the mountains', whilst enjoying a few glasses of wine. They agreed that he had handled the situation fairly well. They were also unanimous in agreeing that skiing was a very dangerous sport and that there had been no forecast of the storm that had engulfed Tom's party. 'We would have done exactly the same as you, Tom. You mustn't fret – your party is back in one piece and that's what matters!'

Later that night, they heard on the news that four people had died in a snowstorm in Verbier, which was situated just across the valley from them. Tom thought, there but for the grace of God...

In all the excitement of the day Tom had had no time to think of anything but getting his party to safety and whether he could have done things better, but before retiring to bed that night and despite feeling both physically and mentally exhausted, he put a telephone call through to Seattle. He wanted to talk to Wendy. After only a little wait while the connection took place, her familiar voice sounded across the miles to Tom in Switzerland. She was more than a little surprised when he said, 'It's just a brief call, darling, just to make quite sure that you're there!'

'Well, you can rest assured that I'm here, as large as life.'
'Wonderful that's all I needed to hear.'
Wendy replied, 'You sound somewhat stressed, Tom? What's up?'

'It's been a bad day, but we're all accounted for and back, safe and sound, in the hotel.'

'I won't ask you for any details right now, but you'll have to tell me later, as you've got me really intrigued!'

'I will, I promise, but as you said, not now.'

'I hope you've had good skiing up until today. I've been thinking about you such a lot this week and wishing I could be there with you,' said Wendy. She had sensed almost immediately how weary Tom was.

'I think you are far better off where you are, darling! I'm flying home the day after tomorrow, so I'll call you on Sunday, when I get back to Wimbledon.'

'Great! I'll look forward to hearing from you. I wasn't expecting you to phone me until you got home, so, for me, this is a real bonus!'

Tom replaced the receiver, undressed and got into bed. He was totally worn out. It was the end of a very long and very exhausting day.

34

'I suggest you take a look at the births, marriages and deaths page in the *Telegraph* on Monday, Tom. I think you'll see something of interest there,' said David as the two men made their way out of Richmond Park to the gates which led out on to Richmond Hill.

It was a bright spring morning and they had decided to have a walk and then go for a drink at a favourite pub of theirs, The Lass of Richmond Hill.

'You dark horse!' exclaimed Tom. 'I bet you've got engaged to Caroline.'

'Yes, indeed I have! I did the dirty deed on Wednesday and we're hoping to get married early in September, maybe October, at the latest,' said David. 'You always said that Caroline found me irresistible, so you were absolutely right!'

'Congratulations!' exclaimed Tom, turning to David and shaking him warmly by the hand. He was genuinely pleased for his friend. 'Are you also going to tell me that I can look forward to a double wedding with Richard and Sarah?'

David laughed before replying, 'Oh, no, I couldn't cope with that! One at a time.'

'Like father, like son – or should it be the other way round? There we were at the New Year, wishing Richard and Sarah a happy Millennium wedding and now it's to be you and Caroline. That's great news, David, well done!'

Tom was somewhat bowled over with David's news. He always imagined David would remain on his own after Jackie's tragic accident. But putting all thoughts of the past aside, Tom was sure that this was the best thing that could happen to David, He was such an easy-going person with a wicked sense of humour and Caroline suited him well.

'I must phone Wendy this evening and give her the news. She'll be thrilled for you! She really liked Caroline and they seemed to have a lot in common as far as their jobs were concerned.'

'No news on that front yet, Tom?' asked David. 'No wedding bells?'

'Not for now,' replied Tom. 'I'm seriously tempted to ask her, but I still need to do a bit of sorting out. To be honest, I've spent all these years being devoted to Nicola and she's given my confidence one hell of a beating. I can't believe how easily she ditched me. One minute I was her rock to lean on, her best friend, her trusted confidant, and then I am ordered to make myself scarce! I am very attracted to Wendy but I need to know that my feelings are for real and that I'm not rushing into the relationship on the rebound from Nicola, I've got to be very sure – one hundred per cent sure!'

'Fair enough. I hear what you're saying, Tom, but remember that Wendy is not Nicola. Wendy is a decent and loving young woman, and what's more, she is besotted with you – but I guess you already know that, without me having to spell it out!'

'Yes, I know you're absolutely right about Wendy, but this obsession that I had with Nicola has really taken its toll on me. I don't know how I'm going to tackle it in the long run.'

'Go with the flow, dear boy!' said David. 'But don't spend too much time dithering about. Wendy won't hang around forever and she does live on the other side of the Atlantic!'

'You're right. Wendy is everything a woman should be and Nicola in contrast is selfish to the core. Nicola wants it all – a successful husband, two clever children, a beautiful home surrounded by an equally beautiful garden, a busy social life and someone like me on the side – good old reliable Tom, ready to jump at her beck and call, someone who will take her to dinner or a theatre and make her feel good!

David, I know that Wendy is worth Nicola a thousandfold and, yes, I probably will ask Wendy to be my wife, but I still need more time to come to terms with all that's happened to me.'

They continued to exchange their news and views in the Lass, over glasses of ice-cold lager.

'When are you off to Seattle? Your visit must be getting pretty near.'

'In a fortnight's time,' replied Tom. 'My flights are booked and I'm staying with the Donald family for five days. I'm really looking forward to it, not only seeing Wendy and her parents, but also Seattle.'

'You tell Wendy that she'll be receiving an invite to our wedding and that she'd better accept – we'd love her to be there.'

'I certainly will and I'm sure she'll want to be there,' replied Tom.

Later in the evening, Tom telephoned David's good news to Wendy and, as he had thought, she was really pleased for them. For a long while after the phone call, Tom sat in his study, complete with a cup of coffee, and settled himself down to do a bit of serious thinking.

Was it really Nicola who was preventing him from making a commitment to Wendy or had he become too used to living on his own after all these years? Perhaps he couldn't see himself as a married man and having to consider someone else, instead of doing his own thing. He'd cared about Nicola for such a long, long time – it was nearly fourteen years since his adoration had begun, and now it was over he'd been forced to rethink his life, without Nicola being a part of it. In the end, Nicola had dropped him like a hot brick, but he still didn't hate her for what she had done to him. His thoughts still centred around her from time to time, but now Wendy had come into his life like a breath of fresh air and he was thankful that she had.

'Damn Nicola! Damn that self-centred woman!' said Tom out aloud, as he finally got up from his chair and made his way upstairs to bed. But Tom knew, despite all his thinking and all his reasoning, that he was still no nearer to solving the dilemma in which he now found himself.

35

The great day had arrived! The plane touched down with only the slightest bump at Seattle-Tacoma Airport and Tom was up and off the plane as soon as possible. He still had the long journey up and down and along various walkways into the immigration hall, where he joined the queue to have his passport scrutinized and his visitor's visa cleared. After a further wait, he was able to collect his luggage off the carousel and make his way through customs. Then, at last, he was able to go to the terminal hall, where Wendy would be waiting to meet him. It took under an hour but for Tom this was far too long.

Tom saw Wendy before she spotted him. She was standing by the exit, straining her neck in order to study every passenger as they got nearer to her. As soon as he saw her, he could sense her excitement.

When she did see him coming towards her in the crowd, her whole face lit up and she waved to him. Tom smiled and waved back. What a different Wendy he was seeing now compared to the one he had seen off to Scotland on New Year's Day! Then she had been really down in the dumps at having to say her goodbyes, and now she was thrilled at being able to say hello to him, and it made Tom feel good.

Tom reached the gate and Wendy literally flung herself into his arms, nearly knocking him over in the process.

'Steady on, darling!' exclaimed Tom, regaining his balance. 'You'll have us in a heap on the floor!'

'I don't care,' replied Wendy. 'It's wonderful to see you and to have you all to myself for five days!'

Tom found Wendy's greeting irresistible and he held her close for a long time, before eventually drawing back from their embrace in order to kiss her on the lips. Tom knew that, at this moment in time, he was as pleased and excited as she was at their being together again.

Tom picked up his suitcase and holdall and let Wendy lead him out of the airport and to the car park where she had left her car.

After a drive of about twenty minutes, Wendy drew up at a house in a pretty, wide, tree-lined avenue. 'This is it, Tom,' she said, as she parked her car in the drive of a large very attractive half-timbered house. It was set back from the road in an open-plan garden, consisting of meticulously mown lawns with manicured edges to them and a long footpath going through the middle, which led up to the front door.

'Home sweet home! Come on, let's go in and say hello to Mom and Dad – they've really been looking forward to your visit.'

If Tom had been a member of the royal family, he couldn't have received a warmer welcome. Enid and Geoff Donald were the perfect hosts and Tom immediately felt at home in their beautiful surroundings. They showed him around and in the evening their neighbours from each side were invited in to meet their visitor from England and to have dinner with him.

As much as Tom had enjoyed the evening, he was more than ready to get to bed as the jet lag, plus the eight-hour time difference, was well and truly kicking in. So while they were all still talking and enjoying an after-dinner drink with their coffee, Tom excused himself.

'Not to worry, Tom,' said Geoff. 'We all understand. After all, it's six o'clock in the morning for you. Even though we were going in the other direction we felt exactly the same when we came over to the UK for New Year. The travelling and the time change throws your body and mind way out of routine, but you'll be fine after a good night's sleep, my boy.'

Tom bade his goodnights and made his way up to his room. The guest room was inviting and warm. The bed covers had already been turned down for him, and a bath towel and a hand towel were neatly folded on a chair with a bar of soap and some shower gel on the top of them. Tom felt completely at ease with the Donald family, who had gone out of their way to make him so very welcome.

Tom got into bed and just savoured lying there for a while. The last twenty-four hours had been very tiring, to say the least, but it had been worth all the travelling just to see Wendy again. She looked so very attractive this evening; her hair shone, her green eyes sparkled with happiness and her complexion was as smooth and clear as he remembered. If Tom had ever doubted his feelings for her, today all doubts had been done away with.

Lying there in the comfortable bed, Tom remembered how he had felt in Crans Montana when he had spent that traumatic skiing day with the students and how, when it was all over, he had felt an urgent need to speak to Wendy, just to hear her voice and to know she was alive and well. Looking at her today, feeling the warmth of her arms around him, he knew beyond any doubt why he had had that need.

Tom lay there happy and content to be staying in a home where love abounded and where he could look forward to spending some time in the company of this lovely American family, but suddenly tiredness took over and he dropped off into a sound sleep.

36

Tom found the city of Seattle an exciting, wonderful place and he could feel the energy of the people. Situated on the inlets of Puget Sound, in the green countryside of Washington State, with the snow-capped Olympic and Cascade mountains looming in the background, it was a truly majestic setting.

Wendy wasted no time in taking Tom along to Seattle's Waterfront, with its lively mix of shops, restaurants, cruises and other attractions. They ate lunch at one of the famous seafood restaurants and Tom was intrigued by all the fish stalls and chandlers on the front. The whole area was a hive of activity. They watched the various ferry boats going to a variety of places and then went on to Pier 59 for the Seattle Aquarium, where they watched octopus, sharks, eels, seals and salmon.

'I told you I'd take you to the Seattle Aquarium,' said Wendy with a smile. 'You said there wasn't time to visit the one in London, so here we are!'

'And very good it is, too,' replied Tom, who remembered only too clearly how Wendy was somewhat disappointed that they had run out of time in London. The aquarium in Seattle more than compensated – it was really fascinating with all the different species of fish in the tanks.

Afterwards, they visited Pike Place Market, which was just off the Waterfront. America's oldest working market, its nooks and crannies presented every kind of shop and stall, selling everything – antiques, handmade jewellery, colourful sweaters, wood carvings – but perhaps the brightest displays were by the local farmers with their fresh fruit and vegetables and the fishmongers with every kind of seafood, including the North-West salmon in pride of place. 'Isn't it colourful? All those little cafés and a multitude of craft shops,' said Wendy. 'I think the Waterfront has got to be my favourite part of Seattle.'

'I've got to admit, it's got a terrific atmosphere about it, but I'm really looking forward to visiting the most famous symbol of Seattle – the Space Needle, all six hundred and seven foot of it!'

'That's on our list, I promise you,' said Wendy.

'One of my clients told me all about it, as soon as I told her I was visiting Seattle. She said that a visit to the top to the revolving restaurant and the observation deck is amazing. She actually saw it first way back in 1962 when the World Fair was here.'

'Long before my time then,' teased Wendy, who had been born while the World Fair was on. 'But even so, I must be a mind reader. I've already reserved us a table for tomorrow's lunch in that very restaurant. You'll love the views across the city to the mountains. Mount Rainier really dominates the scene.' Then she added amid more laughter, 'And no, you're not going across to them to ski!'

'As if I would!' replied Tom. 'How could such a thought ever go through my mind? But the trip to the Needle sounds pretty romantic to me.'

Tom put his arm around Wendy's slim waist and they continued on their walkabout. He felt completely relaxed in Wendy's company, just as he had done in London. They talked away nonstop, savouring every minute of their time together.

'Did you ever get to see the film *Sleepless in Seattle*?' asked Wendy.

'Indeed I did,' replied Tom, remembering that he had taken Nicola to see it. 'I saw it up in Leicester Square, soon after it was released. Tom Hanks made a real hit in it and Meg Ryan played the part of Annie Reed very convincingly. Most of the women in the audience had their tissues out by the end! When I saw the film, little did I know that I would be visiting Seattle – and feeling somewhat sleepless myself.'

Wendy laughed, and stopped to give Tom an unexpected hug before saying, 'When we're sightseeing tomorrow, we'll go over to Union Lake and I'll show you the house boats. One of them was where the Tom Hanks character lived – you know, Sam!'

'I shall look forward to it, darling!'

'Tom, thanks for coming to see me. I really mean it – Seattle is a long way from England and you've come for such a short time and there's lots of travelling involved. You've no idea how much I've been looking forward to your visit!'

'And thank you for making me so very welcome, darling, and that goes for your parents as well. They're a great couple!'

'The pleasure is ours, Tom, I can assure you. I didn't realize in January just how much I was going to miss you, and I've been counting the days to your visit.'

'Me, too,' replied Tom, and now it was his turn to take Wendy into his arms. It felt so good to hold her pressed to the contours of his body and he was barely aware of the passers-by who stared at them. The two of them were cocooned in their own special world – a very exclusive world that belonged to a man who lived on one side of the Atlantic Ocean and a woman who lived on the other. But, nevertheless, they were a man and a woman who needed one another.

Tom knew whilst standing on the Waterfront in Seattle, holding Wendy as he was, that without a shadow of a doubt he was in love with her – and it was not on the rebound, not as a consolation, but for real.

37

'Wendy, correct me if I'm wrong, but doesn't Seattle consider itself to be the coffee capital of the world?'

'It sure does!' replied Wendy and continued, 'It has more coffee shops and types of coffee than anywhere else. The joke is, it's sometimes difficult to get just an ordinary cup of coffee when you want one!'

'That's exactly what I'd heard,' said Tom, who was emptying a sachet of sugar into his cappuccino at the end of an excellent lunch in the Space Needle's restaurant. 'What fabulous views from up here!'

'Great, aren't they! I knew you wouldn't fail to be impressed. Forget the food, just admire the views!'

'The food is pretty impressive, too,' said Tom, and promptly ordered another coffee. 'What's on our agenda, Madam Chairperson, for this afternoon?'

'Well, immediately below the Needle is the Seattle Centre, which also grew out of the World's Fair. There's the Opera House, the Pacific Science Centre, the Children's Museum and various theatres, so, if you like, I'll give you a conducted tour of them all and you can see what's on offer.'

'Sounds great to me, darling!' said Tom, who had had his second cup of coffee placed before him.

'Tom, forgive me for asking, or maybe you'd call it prying, but how come some gorgeous lady hasn't pinned you down by now – not that you can hear me complaining. If this American lady finds you so darn attractive, how do you hold the English ones at bay?' asked Wendy a little nervously, placing her hand over her heart.

'Bit complicated to explain, and you've put me on the spot,' replied Tom, who knew it was only a question of time before Wendy would want to tackle him on the age-old subject. He'd half wondered if Judi had told her, remembering that he talked to her about Nicola on their Canadian holiday. 'But the answer to your first question is – no, I don't mind you asking and no, I don't think you're prying. The answer to your second question is that I foolishly became besotted with a married woman. Don't ask me how it all began, because it all happened a very long time ago. It wasn't some sordid affair either. It was more like a deep, obsessive, friendship. The lady in question, Nicola, had a husband who continually cheated on her and I just happened to be the person that was happy to be there for her. We enjoyed each other's company whenever she could get some time away. It wasn't always easy as she has twins – a boy and a girl – who are coming up seventeen. But it's all over now, Wendy. I haven't seen or spoken to her since last summer. Nicola decided last year, when I came back from the week in the Rockies, that my services were no longer required.'

'Poor you! She must have hurt you, and I know, only too well, what it's like to be hurt! I was engaged for a time to this guy called Mitch when I lived in Boston. I was working as the feature editor on a women's magazine and Mitch was the manager of a motel. We lived together for ages and then, right out of the blue, no warning at all, he announced that he was moving out and that marriage was not his scene! He wasted no time in packing his cases, and within twenty-four hours he'd fled the nest. I felt terrible, it was the last thing I'd expected to happen.'

Tom looked across the table deep into Wendy's eyes and reached across for her hand, giving it a squeeze before saying, 'Well, the way I look at it now, darling, is that if I was still making myself available for Nicola and you were still engaged to Mitch, you and I wouldn't be together today sharing our lunch at the top of Seattle's Space Needle! I love being with you, Wendy – you are the best thing that's happened for me in a long, long time, and forgive me if that sounds a bit corny.'

'Tom, darling, the feeling is mutual, I can promise you! It's no good any of us clinging on to the past, it doesn't get you anywhere. It only festers and makes you bitter and resentful. I tried it for a while, but I slowly learnt that I had got to live for the present and look forward to the future. It's really the only way to live as none of us can turn the clock back – and meeting you is the greatest!'

'Thanks, darling. So, let's raise our glasses and drink a toast "To us and to whatever the future has in store!"'

'Do you realize that tomorrow is Easter Sunday?' asked Tom, putting his glass down.

'I sure do!' replied Wendy. 'What's more, we've guests arriving for brunch. Mom has invited them for eleven o'clock, and so I guess we'll eat around midday. I'll make you a coffee when you come downstairs and I might even let you have a home-made cookie with it!'

Tom laughed and said, 'I can see I'm going to have to work doubly hard at getting myself into my fitness mode when I get back home. You've been plying me with all this good food since I arrived and, at this rate, it will be my clients reading me the riot act!'

'Not to worry – it's not every week that you come over to sample the American way of life,' said Wendy. 'Come on, Tom, let's go and explore some more. First stop – the Opera House!'

38

The twenty-third of April – Easter Sunday – dawned bright and fine. Tom came downstairs after a good night's sleep and was greeted by a wonderful aroma of freshly brewed coffee.

Wendy was already busying herself in the kitchen with her mother. He saw that she was wearing the emerald green trouser suit which he had so much admired in London. When Wendy saw him, she put down a tray full of waffles and went straight over to him. As though it was the most natural thing to do, she put her arms around his neck and kissed him long and meaningfully on his lips. For a split second, Tom wondered what Enid would make of her daughter's outward display of affection, but she just carried on beating some eggs up in a large mixing bowl. When Wendy drew back to catch her breath, she said, 'Good morning, Tom. Happy Easter!'

'Good morning, darling, and a very happy Easter to you. I wish the same to you, Enid. Happy Easter,' said Tom walking over to her and giving her a kiss on both cheeks.

'Morning, Tom. Help yourself to a mug of coffee off the stove. There's a jug of cream in the fridge, or milk, if you'd prefer it. I'm afraid you've a little while to wait for brunch, but our friends should be arriving in a couple of hours and then we can eat.'

'That's fine by me, Enid, but there must be something I can do to help. I've become pretty domesticated living on my own for all these years.'

'Thanks for the offer, but everything is organized. Why don't you and Wendy take a walk around the block? It's a wonderful morning and everything is under control in the kitchen.'

'Fine, just as long as you're sure that I can't help. How about it, Wendy – are you up for a power walk?'

'I certainly am! Just let me get my trainers on and then we'll go. You finish your coffee.'

An hour later they arrived back indoors. The walk had been great and it had given Tom plenty of time to look at the surroundings. He was impressed. The houses in the vicinity were all rather grand, they were open-plan, as was the Donald's house, and everywhere was spacious – wide streets and vast green lawns. Tom guessed it was a good area to live.

'Who's coming for brunch, Wendy?' asked Tom as Wendy poured him out a large glass of mineral water and then one for herself.

'Some friends of my mom's. You'll like them, Tom, they're a great couple and we'll have a good laugh.'

'Right, I'm going up to shower and change before they arrive. See you in a while,' said Tom.

Tom was coming downstairs half an hour later when he heard a car pull up in the driveway and in a couple of minutes the doorbell was sounding. He had gone into the kitchen to refill his glass, then heard the guests' voices in the hall – those of James and Judi! Tom came out of the kitchen and there were his friends – as large as life – greeting Enid and Wendy. Tom was really taken aback by their appearance – it was a wonderful surprise. Tom turned to Wendy and said, 'How on earth did you manage to fix this all up – I never guessed a thing!'

'Easy!' replied Wendy. 'I did it ages ago with Judi when I returned from my New Year trip to the UK. I just kept my fingers crossed that you would definitely come to Seattle for Easter!'

'Great stuff!' exclaimed Tom. He was more than a little pleased to see his friends from Vancouver and appreciated all the planning involved in organizing their visit. What's more, Wendy knew what their friendship meant to Tom and she had done all this for him.

'We've had a good drive down here, we've clocked just

over a hundred miles and done it in two and a half hours door to door,' said James.

'Well done, the both of you,' said Wendy. 'Now come on into the lounge and meet my dad and I'll get you a drink – I expect you're gasping! What's it to be – coffee or something stronger?'

'I'd like a long drink of Coke with some ice in,' said James, and Judi was quick to second the request.

'Two Cokes with ice coming on up,' replied Wendy.

'Thanks. It's great seeing you guys again,' said Judi. She'd been so looking forward to the visit.

Tom knew he wouldn't be forgetting Easter Day 2000 in a hurry – it was a fantastic day and he was touched that Wendy and her mother had planned it for his benefit. It was another way in which Wendy was wanting to show her love for him and he appreciated it. Wendy was one of life's givers and it had made her the lovely person she was today.

Easter brunch was spent eating, drinking, talking, laughing and reminiscing, not to mention forward planning!

'So we're all agreed? We'll try and book up for the Alaskan cruise for the last week in July?' said Enid as she sliced up a pecan pie and an apple pie for family and guests.

'We're all agreed, Enid,' replied James, who had taken it on himself to do all the bookings. 'It is now firmly on the top of my list marked "things to do"! The ship will sail from Vancouver and so it's on our doorstep – leave it to me!'

39

The day when Tom would have to fly home arrived all too soon. His flight wasn't until the early evening, so they spent the day relaxing, packing and a little bit of last-minute shopping and, at Tom's request, lunch in the Space Needle.

Wendy proved to be quiet throughout the meal and Tom detected, as he had done in London, that it was due to her having to say goodbye to him yet again. Their next scheduled meeting was to be the Alaskan cruise at the end of July.

'Cheer up, darling,' said Tom. 'You know I don't like seeing you down in the doldrums. The holiday will soon come round and we'll be together again – it's something we can plan and look forward to.'

'You're right, I know, but it still doesn't make the parting any easier. July still seems a heck of a long time off to me and I just don't want you to go back home – it's as simple as that! You've no idea how much I'd been looking forward to spending this Easter with you, and now it's all over and we'll be at the airport at four o'clock ready for your flight. I guess I've got every reason to be down in the dumps.'

'I'm not exactly relishing the prospect myself, darling. It's been a wonderful five days here with you and your family in "sleepless" Seattle, but now we've got the Alaskan cruise to go on in twelve weeks' time – so hang on to that and you'll be fine.'

Tom sensed how close to tears Wendy had become. He was on the verge of asking her to become engaged to him before he returned home, but, as usual, when it came to it, he couldn't bring himself to do it. It was as though something, or someone, was stopping him. Tom knew he'd regret it later, as this could be the perfect time and place to ask her and he was pretty sure that Wendy would say yes. But right now, his head was ruling his heart and he couldn't go any further than think about it.

The moment passed and they continued their general conversation. Tom wondered whether Wendy had sensed that he was on the brink of proposing to her, but looking over at her, she didn't give anything away and maybe she had been none the wiser. Tom hoped so.

Tom had made it abundantly clear over the last few days how deep his feelings were. There had been one particular evening when they had lain in each other's arms and he had confessed his love for her. She, in return, had told him that she was in love with him, beyond any shadow of doubt. What in heaven's name was holding him back? Had Nicola destroyed his confidence in the opposite sex completely? Was he frightened of being rejected? In the normal way, Tom was brimming over with self-confidence in each and every aspect of his life, but, strangely enough, he found himself lacking confidence where Wendy was concerned.

They arrived at Seattle Airport promptly at four o'clock. Enid and Geoff had wanted to come along with their daughter to see Tom off. Tom guessed that they were partly there to give their daughter some moral support as they would have picked up on her melancholy. After Tom's luggage had been checked in and he'd been issued with his boarding pass, they went off to find a coffee shop where they could relax until his flight to London was called.

Enid said kindly, 'Tom, we've really enjoyed having you as our house guest over the Easter holiday and we want you to know that you'll always be welcome if you'd like to stay with us again.'

'Thanks, Enid. I might well take you up on your offer. Seattle is a fascinating city and I'd love to explore some more of it. Thank you for giving me such a great time – it'll be an Easter that I won't forget in a hurry!'

Tom's gate for boarding was announced over the Tannoy system and the Donald family walked with him to the departure point. Tom was conscious of silent tears rolling down Wendy's cheeks and he kicked himself again for not having had the guts to propose to her earlier on when they were alone. It was his own stupid fault – he should have given her the reassurance she needed. He reached out and drew her into his arms and held her.

'Darling, please don't get so upset – I don't want to leave you like this! I promise you that we'll soon be together again and then we'll make up for lost time.'

'Sorry, Tom,' said Wendy, sobbing. 'I can't seem to help myself. All the way to the airport I kept telling myself that I mustn't cry, but I can't stop! I hate goodbyes at the best of times, but saying them to you is the worst possible scenario – sorry!'

'Just remember that I love you, and all the distance in the world is not going to alter that fact.' Tom gave her a gentle loving kiss on her lips and a final hug before turning to bid his farewells to Enid and Geoff. Finally he said to them, 'It's been a great holiday and thanks for being such super hosts. I'm already looking forward to seeing you on the twenty-second of July! Meantime, please take great care of Wendy for me.'

And with that last remark, Tom walked swiftly through into the passport control area. He couldn't even bring himself to turn round and wave. He was feeling choked up at having to say goodbye to the wonderful American family who had made him so welcome.

Damn, damn, damn, thought Tom during his flight home. What's the matter with me? Wendy is everything I need, everything I want, and I go and mess it up! It would have been so simple to have asked her to be my wife, but no, that would have been too easy, so instead, I ruin it all. What the hell is the matter with me? Tom's thoughts continued to spin round and round in his mind. He was hardly aware of the passing of time on the journey, although he did eventually drift off for a few hours' sleep.

David was there to meet him at Heathrow, complete with Caroline, and her presence somehow added to his discomfort. David and Caroline were a couple – an item – Tom was arriving back home alone, and it could have been so different. He could have been in the same position as David and Caroline – two people who loved each other and were busy planning their future together.

Tom was arriving home with plenty of happy memories of an Easter spent in Seattle, but the woman he loved was still out there. If Wendy had by now analysed their situation, she would more than likely be wondering why Tom hadn't asked her to marry him – he had told her enough times how much he loved her. For a moment he hated himself for having been so insensitive to Wendy's feelings – he'd had plenty of chances and he'd blown them.

40

Back at home, Tom quickly immersed himself in his work. Even though he had only been away a few days, the answerphone was full of calls to follow up and there seemed to be a pile of mail which needed sorting and answering. He had also promised various clients that he would get in touch as soon as he returned and it took time to establish contact with them.

Tom did, however, find time to send off a short thank-you note to Seattle to thank Enid and Geoff and of course Wendy for making his stay with them such fun. Tom had no difficulty with this letter because, apart from his present concern that he had not said all he wanted to say to Wendy, he had enjoyed every minute of his stay. In a sense though it was rather a formal note, written out of normal politeness to one's hosts, and so Tom was delighted to receive an e-mail from Wendy just a few days after his return. In it she again expressed her disappointment that Tom had had to return to England but she gave no indication that she felt let down by the way Tom had or had not acted during his stay. Most of her letter was chatty and cheerful and Tom enjoyed it even more as it was about people he now knew and places he had visited. Tom replied in the same light-hearted way and they exchanged regular notes in the same vein over the next few weeks. Both, however, were quite clearly counting down the time to the Alaska cruise and almost always finished off their letters with 'only ... weeks to go'.

The cruise was still three weeks away when Tom heard some surprising news. He was working out with his friend and client Jane Shepherd, and they were chatting about nothing in particular when the subject of how small the world was and how easily people went abroad came up. It was at this point that Jane said, 'You know Graham and Nicola Ross, don't you?'

'I most certainly do,' said Tom, wondering what on earth was coming next.

'Oh,' said Jane, 'I know one of Graham's aunts and she told me that he had been offered a fantastic job at one of the big hotels in Sydney, near Bondi Beach. I don't know much about it, but the whole family just suddenly upped sticks and moved within the last month to Australia.' Jane chatted on about how easy it was to move nowadays, about whether it would upset the children's education, whether Graham's wife would be able to find a job, how nice it would be to live in the sun, but Tom was only half listening, his concentration was definitely waning.

Tom's mind was racing around. He tried to think what he would have done if Nicola had telephoned him and said she needed him because she was not going to Australia, but all he could think now was that he wouldn't have let anything or anyone interfere with his visit to Wendy. He knew he had loved Nicola, but that was in the past and he could only think of the future. Now Nicola was really well and truly out of his life and he was glad of the fact.

At which point he heard Jane say, 'You must really be looking forward to your Alaskan holiday and all that wonderful scenery you're going to see,' and Tom came back to earth again with the firm knowledge that he was really, really looking forward to his holiday and not just for all the sightseeing in Alaska! He knew that it was Wendy he wanted to spend the rest of his life with and that Nicola presented no competition whatsoever.

Tom continued putting Jane though her paces and inwardly was grateful to her for having given him the news of Nicola's departure from England. It made him feel good – it was a clean ending to a long emotional episode in his life, which needed to be put away in the archives of his memory.

41

Tom flew out to Vancouver two days prior to the cruise, to stay with James and Judi. If there was any jet lag to contend with, his friends wanted to make sure that he got it over and done with in Vancouver, so, as Judi put it, 'You can be bright-eyed and bushy-tailed on the cruise!'

As it happened, Tom appreciated their thoughtfulness but, fortunately, the jet lag that he experienced was pretty mild. Even so, he needed to address it and get it out of the way. He wanted to be at his best for the holiday – not to mention for Wendy!

Also, as the cruise was only for a week, Tom would have a little extra time with James and Judi before meeting up with Wendy and her parents prior to sailing.

Tom watched the Donald family arrive by cab. They had arranged to meet up with them at the docks in one of the huge embarkation sheds before boarding the ship – the *Sea Princess*. Tom's anticipation at seeing Wendy was all consuming. He experienced feelings of excitement, nervousness, apprehension, but the love he felt for her was as strong and as real as before. He'd blamed himself over and over again, for 'messing up' at Easter – Wendy must have wondered what on earth he was playing at, one minute he was telling her how much he loved her and the next minute he was flying back to England without giving her any words of assurance of a real commitment. He must have been crazy, but he knew himself well enough to realise that he had to be one hundred per cent sure.

Wendy saw Tom standing waiting to meet them, and, while her father was settling up with the cab driver, rushed over to embrace him. It felt so good to feel her in his arms once more, her body pressing hard up against his, and any doubts Tom may have felt regarding what Wendy's feelings were immediately blown right away.

Tom was the first to speak. 'Darling, I haven't seen you in twelve weeks, but the last few minutes have been the longest!'

Wendy replied, 'It's been the same for me, especially knowing that you've been here, in Vancouver for the last forty-eight hours. So near, but so far!' She paused for a while to embrace first Judi and then James. 'Oh, it's so good to see you both – Easter Sunday seems a heck of a long time ago!'

With great gusto, Wendy turned around to hug Tom yet again. 'Tom, this is the moment I've been willing to happen ever since I saw you off in Seattle! I can't believe it's all happening!'

'Come on, you two love birds – you'll have plenty of time for romance when we get on board ship,' said James, who was anxious to get the official boarding completed.

They were shown to their prospective cabins, which were situated on deck eleven, conveniently next door to one another. Their four outside cabins were all served by the same steward – George – a very likeable young man, who told them that he would be happy to be at their beck and call for the week's cruise. 'Just pick up your telephone receiver and dial 123 and I'll be at your service.'

'Sounds a bit like rubbing the magic lamp and the genie appears,' said James teasingly, having taken an instant liking to this young Mexican steward who was obviously so willing to please his passengers.

'Absolutely, sir!' replied George, smiling at him. 'Now, in an hour's time there is going to be a fire drill – all passengers and crew have to attend. You will be directed to your muster stations, and please take your life jacket along with you – you'll find it on the top shelf of your wardrobe.'

'Let's hope we won't be needing them for real,' said Enid, with memories of the *Titanic* film not so far away.

The unpacking and the fire drill over with, they met up

on deck to enjoy a rum cocktail, sitting by the swimming pool in glorious sunshine. 'This is the life!' said Geoff, stretching himself out on a recliner. 'The cocktail is excellent and the sunshine is even better. I guess I could force myself to enjoy the week ahead!'

'Hear, hear!' replied Enid. 'I second that. What time did you say the ship is due to sail?'

'It's scheduled for five o'clock,' replied James, and he'd no sooner said the words than there was an announcement made from the bridge.

'The ship's departure has been delayed, owing to the fact that seventy-five passengers are stranded in Chicago due to dreadful weather conditions!'

After dinner, at nine thirty, the *Sea Princess* set sail, and the trip to Alaska had begun. The six of them had been allocated a good table in one of the ship's formal restaurants. As they were a unit of six, they were given their own table, without having to share with any fellow passengers. This suited them – not because they were unsociable, but because it was much nicer to be able to share their shipboard dinners within their own party.

Next stop from the dining room they visited the ship's theatre and watched a show which they found a real waste of space. Top of the bill was a so-called comedian. 'How do they call him a comedian when he isn't even funny?' asked Tom. 'I reckon someone will have him overboard by the end of the cruise!'

After the show they agreed that it was time to catch up with some sleep – it was fast approaching midnight and it had proved a long day. They bade their goodnights and went off to their cabins, agreeing to meet up for breakfast in the Horizon restaurant at eight thirty the following morning.

Tom lay in bed, vaguely conscious of the ship's movement, thinking about Wendy. His feelings were running high and he was tempted to phone her cabin. He wanted to see her and to hold her, but thought better of it; despite his desire, he needed to sleep. It was still necessary for Tom to pace himself and the last two or three days had been pretty hectic and he felt weary – happy but weary. His love for Wendy could wait, but his need for sleep couldn't.

42

The next morning, they met up as planned for their breakfast. They looked out of the huge picture windows as they sailed along, enjoying their food. Wendy was the first to observe a couple of whales diving in and out of the sea.

'Look, everyone!' she said excitedly. 'Aren't they lovely? You see them in films, but to see them for real, just has to be something else.'

After breakfast they sat out on deck, but found it too cold after only a short time. They decided to go inside and down a few decks to have a look around the ship's shops, which were situated on the purser's deck. Also, they could enjoy a cup of coffee in the lounge there.

Their first day was spent finding their way around this vast ship and they cruised the whole day. Tom found that being with Wendy was as stimulating as before and they revelled in each other's company. Their love, which had grown steadily deeper over the last year, was plain for all to see. Enid and Geoff knew, beyond a shadow of a doubt, that their daughter had fallen for Tom, hook, line and sinker. And they liked what they saw.

Before dinner that night, the captain of the ship gave his traditional welcoming cocktail party, when he wished all his passengers bon voyage. It was both a good end to their first day and a formal start to their cruise, and they spent an enjoyable evening.

The following morning, the ship docked at Ketchikan, which was their first port of call, and the passengers had the morning to go ashore, when they could do their own thing or go on a pre-booked excursion. Wendy and her mother had booked an excursion which promised that they would see bears in their natural habitat and they were really looking forward to the trip. It was really a big disappointment when they heard the announcement at breakfast that the excursion had been cancelled because of the bad weather. Judi and the men had chosen to go on a float plane trip to see some of the dramatic scenery of the Misty Fjords National Monument wilderness preserve. That was still on, so Tom had the bright idea that he should swop with Enid. At first Enid was reluctant to deprive Tom of his sightseeing but she quickly realized that he was probably keener to have a few hours on his own with Wendy, and so she agreed to go.

So the four travellers set off after breakfast to be taken to where the float planes were. The flight was rather cloudy and dull, so unfortunately they did not see much, but when they landed on a lake, the sun was shining and the water was calm and tranquil. They were able to get out on the wing and the floats of the plane and then go ashore for a walk in some woodlands that surrounded the lake. It was all very beautiful and they felt they were explorers seeing uncharted land for the first time. Meantime, Wendy and Tom were content to explore the ship further, to sit in the lounge, to drink coffee and to talk, but most of all they enjoyed just being together. They didn't have time to notice the weather!

By the afternoon everyone had returned to the ship and it set sail for its next port of call. Next day, they awoke coming in to dock in Juneau, the capital of Alaska. It looked wet and desolate and very uninviting! 'We've obviously left the sunshine behind in Vancouver,' said Wendy. 'Look at that wretched rain!'

'You're right, darling. Not to worry, we'll catch a bus into town and have a good look round,' replied Tom, and added, 'we ought to take a couple of umbrellas – we're about to get soaked.' And a good soaking is precisely what they got! The town proved to be a real disappointment, even forgetting the rain.

'How could this place be the capital of Alaska?' asked

Wendy, whose arm was tucked through Tom's as he held the umbrella over them.

'Good point,' he replied. 'Maybe it would look different if it stopped raining!'

'Maybe it'll stop later on, but it looks pretty set in to me,' said Wendy. 'Tom, I'm with you and I'm in love and I'm on holiday, so who cares about the weather or if we do get wet!'

'Well said, darling,' replied Tom, laughing. He stopped them in their tracks and kissed her, slightly awkwardly under the dripping umbrella. 'Have I told you lately that I love you?'

'I guess so. Ten minutes ago, if you need to be reminded!'

Their next destination was the town of Skagway. They received a wake-up call in their cabins at six thirty. They had booked on an excursion and had to be on shore at seven fifteen. A coach was there on the quayside to meet them off the ship and drove them to catch a boat which would take them on a fourteen-mile trip to the city of Haines, renowned for the greatest gathering of bald eagles. By now they had got used to seeing everything through the rain. They were met at the jetty at Haines and directed to a waiting coach, then they were driven around another wet and desolate town. First stop was Haines's museum, then on to the bald eagle exhibition, where Tom and fellow visitors heard a lecture on the wild life of Alaska.

'That was an excellent presentation,' said Tom as they walked around looking at all the stuffed wild animals which were on display around the hall.

'It sure was,' said Wendy, adding, 'I can't get over how lifelike these animals look, especially the bears and the wolves. I wouldn't like to be in here on a dark night – stuffed animals or not.'

'Nor me!' agreed Judi, and laughed. 'Not even to shelter from the rain – I'd rather get wet! Come on, let's get back to the coach. I reckon we've done Haines.'

Back on board the *Sea Princess* and having enjoyed a good buffet lunch in the Horizon, James said, 'I suggest a power walk around the deck would be a good idea. All this rain is making my joints rusty!'

'Excellent idea, James. Are you guys up for it?'

'Agreed!' came the unanimous response.

A steward had told them that if they were to walk three times round the promenade deck, it was equal to one mile. So, armed with that fact, they set off on a five-mile walk.

The next morning they awoke to see the sun rising over a calm sea and the water was as still as a mill pond. The ship had sailed into the majestic Glacier Bay and was now cruising towards the glaciers.

It was announced from the bridge that the park rangers had boarded the *Sea Princess* earlier, and they would be in charge of the day's itinerary and schedule.

After their usual buffet breakfast, Tom and Wendy stood out on deck with Enid and Geoff one side of them and James and Judi on the other. They all watched, in complete awe, as they cruised closer and closer to the glaciers.

Tom felt Wendy give a shiver. He looked round at her and said, 'Are you all right, darling?'

'Sure,' she replied. 'I just feel so moved by the splendour of these glaciers. It's amazing! I've read about the Margerie glacier, but now I'm seeing it with my own eyes – it's unbelievable!'

The glaciers could best be described as in a cul-de-sac. The captain stopped the ship's engines and the passengers stared spellbound at the glaciers and the views that were spread out before them. They listened to the noise that sounded like thunder, as great chunks of ice broke off the glaciers and fell into the sea.

'I've never seen a sight like this in all my life!' exclaimed Enid. 'And I can hardly believe what I'm seeing!'

'Well, you'd better believe it, mom. Because it's all happening out there,' said Wendy, going over to give her a great bearlike hug.

43

The extreme contrast in the weather conditions the following day was unbelievable. They had just witnessed Glacier Bay bathed in beautiful sunshine under a deep blue sky and now, twenty-eight hours later, they were cruising into College Bay watching glacier upon glacier, and it was dull and decidedly overcast. The grey sky was accompanied by an equally grey sea.

As the passengers leant on the ship's rails, eagerly watching the passing sights with their binoculars at the ready, there was a slight swell and patches of mist.

'Where's our sunshine gone again?' asked Wendy, pulling the zip up higher on her fleece. 'It's turned very cold.'

'Never mind, darling. We had our blue skies and sunshine yesterday in Glacier Bay and now it's a totally different atmosphere visiting the glaciers today – I rather like the change.'

'I agree,' said James. 'It's almost alien here.'

'You mean a bit creepy!' exclaimed Judi. 'I wouldn't fancy being stranded out here – we're in the middle of nowhere.'

They watched for a long time as the ship cruised really slowly, so that the passengers could witness again the marvels of nature as they sailed past the glaciers on either side of the ship. Each one had been named after various American universities, such as Harvard and Yale.

'Look over there!' cried Wendy. 'Oh, Tom, look – there are water otters swimming on their backs and they're carrying their babies on their tummies! What a sight!'

'Yes, and they're busy swimming from one block of floating ice to another,' replied Tom.

'What an extraordinary existence,' said Judi. 'Such a

weird way to spend their lives – it's kind of in a different world.'

'I don't suppose it bothers them,' replied James. 'After all, they don't know anything different.'

'Well, I for one, feel as though we are intruding on their solitude,' said Wendy, reaching for Tom's hand and holding it tightly.

'I think I know what you mean, darling. This world of glaciers belongs to them. The vast cruise ships who dare to sail into their domain, each carrying hundreds of people who view them through their binoculars, must prove an unreal distraction for them.'

'You've got to admit that it's eerie up here on deck with the mist swirling around. It's so quiet – the ship's engines have stopped,' said Wendy, moving up even closer to Tom. He in turn put his arm around her.

'Let's hope they'll be able to start them up again when they need to,' said Judi. 'It's so isolated and desolate whichever way you look.'

'I don't think you need worry about the engine, darling. I can assure you that the captain knows what he is doing – this will just be routine to him,' said James, smiling at his wife. 'Do I detect you're a little bit scared?'

'In a word, James – yes! It's the whole feel of the place – it's so unreal.'

'Never mind,' replied James. 'I suggest we go inside now and join Enid and Geoff. They said they'd be in the purser's lounge. We'll have a coffee and a cookie. It's certainly getting a lot colder, so let's make a move.'

Judi looked more than a little relieved at his suggestion and agreed without hesitation.

'That's fine by me. Are you and Tom ready to come inside?' asked Judi.

Tom answered her before Wendy had a chance to speak. 'We'll be along in a short while – you two go on ahead and we'll catch up with you.'

'OK – see you in a while. But don't stay out here and freeze,' replied James, and tucking his arm through Judi's he walked off to the nearest deck's entrance.

Tom and Wendy continued viewing the barren landscape.

'What are you thinking?' asked Tom, one arm around Wendy, his other arm resting on the ship's rail.

'I'm just thinking how very privileged I am to be watching those little water otters swimming happily around in this majestic wilderness. We're miles and miles away from civilization as we know it – in this unique setting – and it's incredible to know that a place like this even exists. It's really magic!'

'That's true, and I know exactly how you're feeling, because I feel the same,' replied Tom. Then he turned Wendy round towards him and cupped her face in his hands. He kissed her gently on the lips, then standing a step back said, 'This is also an exceptional place to tell you how very much I love you.'

'I love you, Tom,' responded Wendy, returning his kiss, but this time it was long and passionate, before she said, 'We've known each other a year now and we've visited some wonderful places together, but in my mind College Bay has got to be the best – and I want to be able to remember just how I feel today, not at the end of the holiday, but for always!'

'I'll second that,' replied Tom. 'And I'm going to make sure you do always remember it, because I'm going to ask you if you will spend the rest of your life with me.'

For what seemed an age Wendy was speechless, but then she said, 'Tom, is that your way of asking me to marry you or what?'

Tom gave her a quick kiss and replied, 'I certainly am! You can forget the "or what" bit! And now you're going to ask me what took me so long?'

'As if I would,' Wendy replied, her whole face alight with happiness. 'Oh, Tom, I feel so happy – please don't ask me to explain 'cos I can't!'

'You don't have to, darling – I couldn't describe it, but it's a great feeling! Now how about giving me that all-important answer to my question?'

'My answer is YES! Tom, I would love to spend the rest of my life with you, in fact, I can't think of a single thing in the world that I'd rather do!'

Tom put his hand inside his jacket pocket and brought out a ring pouch. He opened the drawstring and produced a lovely diamond cluster engagement ring. He took Wendy's left hand and slipped the ring on the appropriate finger and said, 'I love you, Wendy and I always will. Let's arrange to marry this year; 2000 has got to be extra special – we did see the Millennium in together!'

'We sure did,' replied Wendy. 'I knew even then that I wanted to be with you forever and having to say goodbye to you at the airport was the pits!'

'Come on, darling, let's go in and join the others. I can't wait to tell them our news. But remember that I'll need to ask your father's permission to marry his lovely daughter!'

44

Hours later and a great deal of champagne having been consumed, Tom and Wendy sat up in the Horizon lounge to watch the *Sea Princess* slowly approaching Seaward. The crew brought the ship in, manoeuvring round large rocks en route, and the speed reduced to a minimum. They could see the lights of Seaward twinkling in the distance. The ship's engines stopped and they moored off for a while.

'We're obviously a bit too early to get into our berth,' said Tom. 'But it suits me fine – champagne at the ready and with my future wife sitting at my side!'

'Tom,' said Wendy, holding his hand in her lap, 'I want to tell you – and one day, hopefully, our children – that I have never felt so happy in the whole of my life as I do today and tonight. I never imagined that it was possible to love someone as much as I love you. I am so happy right now – it's just unbelievable how happy! I've felt more happiness in the last few hours than I've felt in my entire lifetime, and it's all because of you – wonderful you!'

'Thank you, darling. The feelings I have today are incredible – as long as I have your love, nothing else is as important. We met this time last year, in the Canadian Rockies, and now, a year on, we've got engaged in a bay full of glaciers and water otters in Alaska. We're different – you've got to admit!'

'I admit it! I can hardly believe all that's happened in the last year and I want to ask you a question – when did you first know that I was the one for you? Be honest, I want to know.'

'It was when I was in Switzerland and I had all that drama in the mountains. That particular evening after the eventful day, I was dead tired, I felt threatened and vulnerable by what had happened and I was questioning every incident that had taken place. That night I felt as if I had the cares of the world on my shoulders and yet I couldn't go to bed until I'd phoned you. Once I'd heard your voice, I felt relieved and reassured. I felt safe just knowing you were there, even if you were thousands of miles away – you were there! I knew that night that I needed you, I wanted you and that I loved you, and I decided there and then that, if you'd have me, I would marry you.'

'Then I can ask you that question now – what took you so long?' asked Wendy, sipping her champagne and waiting for Tom's answer.

'I don't even know if I can answer it. I do know that I wanted to ask you before I flew home from Seattle, but I couldn't get it together and I had a lousy flight back home regretting that I hadn't asked you. Maybe I was nervous that you would turn me down, and I don't think I could have coped with that. Wendy, I had to be sure. I'm English, you're American and we're going to have to make adjustments in our life together. Sometime, very soon, we're going to decide where we are going to live, work and bring up our family – and that could present a problem.'

Wendy answered without a moment's hesitation, 'No problem, Tom. I'll live with you anywhere you want me to – just as long as you're by my side, I'd be happy to live in Timbuktu! Really, Tom, I mean it. I'm happy to go along with your choice – if you want to stay in England, that's fine by me. With one proviso – that we visit mom and dad at least twice a year.'

'Well, that's wonderful because I've been thinking, regarding my home, my job etc., it would be best if we lived in Wimbledon. I own my house and I have a regular income from my fitness training business, and now I have other trainers on my team. After all is said and done, I expect to be the breadwinner. So, thank you, darling, we'll just have to work on you becoming a Wimbledon Womble – I'll tell you about them sometime! But let's get married in Seattle

– it will be much easier for your parents to have your family and friends close by and I can hopefully get my closest friends and my sister to fly out for our big day.'

That night they went down to Wendy's cabin. They watched from the cabin's window as the tugs pushed the *Sea Princess* into her berth at Seaward, the cruise's final port of the holiday. The passengers would disembark in the morning and be coached up to Anchorage, then they would fly home to their various destinations.

After witnessing the various activities on the quayside and on the water, they lay down on the bed. Then Tom took Wendy in his arms and they made love. It was the start of their own voyage through life together – a long journey about to be shared as man and wife.

45

Upon reflection, Tom's sixth sense had always known that one day he would see Nicola again. He never quite knew how it would happen, or where, or when, but somehow he just knew they'd meet again – and now they just had.

Over the years – twelve to be precise – Tom had got on with his life and enjoyed a good marriage with Wendy. The obsessive love which he'd had for Nicola had faded naturally into the background as he lived out a busy working and social life. At times he found himself remembering Nicola and wondering what his life would be like now if she hadn't chosen to walk out on him. He guessed that he most probably would have chosen to remain a bachelor – waiting for the phone calls from Nicola, then jumping at the chance to spend some time with her, albeit rationed time.

Although Tom had been bitter when she severed their relationship, he discovered that time had a great way of making the unhappy times less painful and the good times more prominent. He came to the conclusion that it was far easier and simpler to recall kind words from someone, but difficult to remember their harsh words of rejection and betrayal.

When Tom married Wendy, he was forty-eight years old and Wendy was ten years his junior. Now, twelve years on, Tom was celebrating his sixtieth birthday and his wife her fiftieth.

After having spent lengthy discussions as to what to do and how they would like to do justice to their birthdays, they settled for a trip aboard the *Royal Scotsman* – a train journey 'from the past' that would take them from Edinburgh up the West Coast of Scotland, across country and back down the East Coast to return to Edinburgh. Tom had discovered his appetite for train journeys ever since travelling through the glorious Rockies in Canada on that very special tour when he and Wendy had first met.

Tom and Wendy were both ready for a break from their busy lives and this Scottish trip on a luxurious train sounded great. They were two professional people who gave their very best in their chosen careers. Tom had built up a thriving business over the years. He by now employed nine personal fitness trainers on his team, and the business proved both demanding and rewarding. In practice, Tom spent most of his time dealing with administration and liaising with his clients, whilst he left the actual workouts to his trainers.

Wendy also was well established teaching journalism at one of the best-known secretarial colleges in London, in South Kensington. Although her job involved travelling up to town each day, she really enjoyed working with the students. Wendy knew she was providing them with the knowledge they'd need to become newspaper reporters or editors on papers and magazines, and maybe there were some future authors among them. Wendy had a real gift for teaching and her hard work was rewarded by the successes of many of her students.

Since their marriage, Wendy and Tom lived in what had been Tom's house in Wimbledon. Wendy had loved her new home right from the start, and she loved living in the village, which had the added bonus of being close to the Common with all its glorious walks to the windmill and beyond. She had even grown to accept the Fox and Grapes as her 'local', just as Tom and David had before her, and she had fitted into the English way of life with no problems at all. Tom used to say to her, 'Darling, you are to the manor born!' and Wendy would go up, put her arms around him and reply, 'It's only because I love you so very, very much!'

After David married Caroline, they had bought themselves a large three-bedroomed flat overlooking Putney

Heath, and so they lived only a couple of miles away from Tom and Wendy in Wimbledon. The girls had become firm friends and they and their husbands often socialized as a foursome, spending many happy hours together.

With a busy job and an equally busy social life, Wendy had no time to feel homesick. Enid and Geoff had come over to visit many times and they enjoyed the English way of life. They would also combine their visit with a trip up to Scotland to visit Enid's sister, Kate. 'If you hadn't married an Englishman, darling, I'd never have got to see so much of my sister,' said Enid happily.

'Well, there you have it, mom. I did get it right after all,' replied Wendy with a great smile and a wink for her very special mom.

'You certainly did, sweetheart! Your dad and I can feel the happiness that radiates when you and Tom are together. Now I hope you won't mind me asking you a very personal question, or even think that I'm being an inquisitive mom, but I'm going to ask you anyway. Do you and Tom want children?' Her daughter had been married for two years and had recently turned forty.

'Mom, of course I don't mind you asking! It's the most natural thing in the world for a mother to ask her daughter that question! But I'm afraid that I've got to admit defeat in that department. We've been trying for a baby ever since we got married, but nothing has happened, and now I guess that my time clock is beginning to run out. If only I'd married Tom ten years earlier, we might have two or three little ones by now. Anyway, it's no good fretting about what might have been, and I do think that with each passing year it becomes less likely that I'll ever conceive. In the meantime, Tom and I have decided to get on with our lives, and I'm going back into teaching full-time next term. You're not to worry about it, mom, because you've just got to remember that Tom and I have each other to love and to care for and we're both more than happy to settle for that.'

Enid looked over to her daughter and she could only

make a guess at how much Wendy must be hurting inside. She knew what loving parents both Wendy and Tom would have proved, but it looked as though life wasn't going to give them the chance to experience it.

46

Now, ten years on and no children on the scene, Tom and Wendy made their way by taxi from Edinburgh Airport to the Balmoral Hotel on Princes Street It was here that the tour checked in and where they would be greeted by a member of the *Royal Scotsman* crew who would accompany the party throughout the trip.

After having had a drink and meeting up with some of their fellow passengers, they were driven by taxi to Edinburgh's Waverley station to board the train. Wendy was really impressed that they wouldn't see their luggage again until they reached their allotted cabin.

'It reminds me of our cruise to Alaska,' remarked Wendy. 'We didn't see our luggage there on the quayside again until it appeared in our cabins. It must all take some organizing!'

'All part and parcel of the holiday, darling,' said Tom, watching Wendy's excitement growing by the minute.

The train looked smart standing in the platform and there was a piper in full Scottish dress to pipe them on board. Instead of going straight to their cabins, the passengers were asked to go along to the lounge car, where champagne was being served, followed by afternoon tea.

'It's amazing,' said Wendy as she sat in one of the comfortable chairs. 'We could be sitting here in someone's gracious lounge in their stately house, if it wasn't laid out lengthways!'

'It certainly could,' said Tom, sitting down on a corner seat of a settee opposite his wife. There were maroon carpets and matching maroon curtains, and flowers and potted plants everywhere. Little lamps were on the tables placed between the chairs and settees and there were bowls of fruit to add yet more colour to this gracious lounge. Stewards busied themselves with their trays of champagne and bucks fizz to welcome the passengers. They made quite sure that each and everyone had a glass of bubbly, and then made sure it was kept topped up. They had been well trained! Next, scones and cream and jam were served with a choice of tea, and in no time at all, everyone was introducing themselves to one another and the conversation just flowed – it was all very relaxed and easy-going.

There were thirty-four passengers on this particular trip, but only one other couple from England and one couple from Scotland. The rest of the party was made up mostly of Americans and Canadians. Wendy felt well and truly at home amongst her ex-fellow countrymen and she never stopped telling Tom about all the coincidences and people who knew the places and people that she had known in the past.

While they were still enjoying their tea, the *Royal Scotsman* set off and headed west, skirting Glasgow along the northern bank of the Clyde to Craigendoran, which is the starting point for the majestic West Highland Line.

After tea, Tom and Wendy went along with one of the stewards to find their cabin and unpack. Again, like on the cruise, they put their empty cases outside in the corridor for the stewards to store them until they were needed again at the end of their trip.

'The cabins are so well fitted out,' said Wendy, looking around in surprise at the compact area.

'Yes, it amazes me how well they've managed to fit in the shower, a washbasin and a loo in every cabin – and I've discovered that the water is piping hot, so watch out.'

'I will,' said Wendy, adding, 'I'm really glad we don't travel at night – it will be so much nicer to be able to sleep in peace and quiet. I was amused to hear the staff say that the train was "stabled" at night – you'd think we were a train full of racehorses!'

'Yes, it sounds a bit like that! I have a distinct feeling

we're going to enjoy our holiday,' said Tom with a broad smile.

'I second that,' said Wendy. 'We're nearly at Dalmally, according to the programme they've given us. Then we're going by coach to visit Inverawe Smokehouse, where we're going to watch my favourite salmon being smoked!'

The next three days passed in a whirl of travel, sightseeing, gourmet food, excellent wines and convivial company. It proved a perfect mixture for a holiday.

'If you had to give the highlight of the holiday for you, what would you say?' asked Tom as they got changed for their final dinner of the trip.

'I've loved it all, darling, but maybe if I had to choose one in particular, I think the visit to the Isle of Skye – the Misty Isle – has to be my favourite. The wild grandeur of the north down to the lush green scenery of the south appeals to my romantic nature. I loved having my coffee and shortbread sitting at that round table in front of a roaring fire and exchanging small talk with Bob and Sue.'

'I missed out on that when I was battling with the cold and the wind to take some photographs. Just let's hope they'll all come out, as I'd forgone my coffee at the Sligachan Hotel with you.' But Tom was secretly very relieved that Wendy hadn't accompanied him and that he had had some time to himself.

He found it incredible that it was on the remote Isle of Skye, of all places, that he had come face to face with Nicola. It had been more than thirteen years since they had last seen each other, and that was the time when Nicola had severed their relationship for good.

Tom had gone off with his camera, leaving Wendy to enjoy her coffee and to keep warm whilst he went off to search for suitable settings to photograph. He'd walked for about a quarter of a mile or so down the road, crossed over a bridge and climbed up a smallish hill from where he knew he would be able to get some excellent views of Sligachan and the mighty Cuillin Hills. Up on the hill Tom was surrounded by magnificent scenery in every direction.

Although busily absorbed in taking his photographs, Tom noticed a lone figure of a woman climbing up the hill towards him and she was calling out his name. At first, Tom couldn't believe who it was that he was seeing, but, yes, it was definitely Nicola! The nearer she got to him, the more obvious it was that it was her.

When she eventually caught up with him, she was extremely out of breath and she stared at him for a moment or two before saying, 'Tom! I thought it was you! I saw you from my car as I was crossing the bridge, so I parked and set off in pursuit of you. But what on earth are you doing here?'

Tom returned her stare in disbelief – the woman who stood before him was definitely Nicola, but she was desperately thin, her face lined and there was black under her tired eyes. She wore a pair of jeans, and a short camel coat with a matching belt tied tightly round her waist which only emphasized how very thin she was. Her long brown boots appeared to be at least two sizes too big for her. Tom cleared his throat and said, 'Well, I can't believe it's you, Nicola! But in answer to your question, I'm here in Scotland on a short holiday. We're travelling on the *Royal Scotsman* and today's excursion is a visit to the Isle of Skye. And what, might I ask, brings you to this remote neck of the woods?'

'I'm staying for a week at Kinloch Lodge Hotel here on the island with my daughter and son-in-law, complete with two very boisterous grandsons and two equally boisterous Labradors! It was a chance for us all to be together for a whole week, and I'm loving it. They live in St Andrews – my son is a don at the university, and my daughter is married to a local GP there. So my twins have both made their homes in St Andrews and each of them is married to a Scot! Are you travelling on your own, Tom?' Nicola inquired, and Tom was conscious of her eyes regarding him intently.

'No, I'm with Wendy, my wife, and we're on holiday to celebrate our two very special birthdays – my sixtieth and

Wendy's fiftieth,' replied Tom, who was still so taken aback at meeting Nicola that he was finding it quite a struggle to speak.

'I'd heard, via the grapevine, that you were married,' replied Nicola, and then added wearily, 'I hope she makes you happy, Tom.'

'She certainly does that! She's a wonderful lady and I'm totally bowled over by her. We've been married now for twelve years – she's American, very lively, very loving and does me a power of good – I'm a very fortunate man,' said Tom, as if somehow he needed to convince Nicola of his feelings towards Wendy. He guessed his words were hurting her, but he felt he had to say them whether they hurt her or not.

But she wasted no time in answering, 'I'm really pleased for you, Tom. You deserve a good woman – someone who is free to love you unconditionally.' Nicola's eyes moved from watching Tom and she gazed down at the ground.

'Did everything turn out all right for you, Nicola?' asked Tom somewhat apprehensively, but he knew the answer before he'd even asked the question just by looking at her.

'No, not really. But that's another story and I really must get back to the family or else they'll be sending a search party out! I promised them I'd only be out for about half an hour at the most and they do worry about me these days. It's really good to see you again, Tom, after all these years and, more important, to know you're OK. I've often thought about you and wondered what you were doing.' And with those words, Nicola leaned over and gave Tom a quick kiss on his cheek, then she turned and hurried back to where she'd left her car. Tom noticed that she never looked back at him. Just as she'd never looked back all those years ago when she walked out of his life.

47

Tom stood transfixed for a good ten minutes after Nicola had gone. He was left with an intense feeling of surprise and pity. Nicola had aged dramatically; she looked ill, pathetic and uncared for. Whatever had happened to her since he'd last seen her? He imagined that Graham, if he was still around, would be treating her like a second-class citizen, whilst he got on with his gallivanting and his womanizing. Probably nothing had changed much for Nicola, except now she had lost her looks and possibly her health. But still, it was no good just imagining what had happened; Tom would probably never know, and he knew it was best for everyone if in fact he didn't. Nicola was his past, Wendy was his present and his future, and Tom couldn't afford to rock the boat in any way whatsoever. His life was good, busy and he was extremely happy married to Wendy – and that's the way he wanted it to remain. It was also many years since he had had his bypass operation, and even his heart had behaved impeccably since then.

When Tom got back into the coach ready for their journey back to Kyle, where the train was waiting, Wendy was already in her seat. She looked up from a brochure she was reading when Tom slipped into the seat beside her.

'Hello, darling. Did you manage to take any good shots? You seem to have been gone for ages – I was just wondering whether I ought to come and look for you! I thought you'd manage to come into the hotel for a coffee.'

Tom replied, 'Sorry I've been so long, darling, but I ended up having to walk quite a way to photograph the scenes I wanted to get, and so we'll just have to hope they'll come out all right. It's pretty bleak outside and I think it's trying to rain. I can imagine how desolate and grim it would be here in the depth of winter – it's not that clever now in early September!' Tom was trying his best to sound as normal and natural as possible, despite the fact that he was feeling somewhat shell-shocked since the encounter he'd had with Nicola. 'Did you have a nice coffee?'

'I certainly did! I sat with Sue and Bob. Isn't it great that they come from Portland in Oregon? They've made me promise to let them know when we're next over in the States and then, hopefully, we can arrange to meet up again. It's a beautiful drive down from Seattle, through Washington State, by Mount St Helens and the Cascades and along the Columbia River – should be fun!'

'I'll look forward to it,' replied Tom. 'It's funny how you just happen to click with certain couples when you first meet, and it happened for us with them.'

Tom couldn't help smiling to himself as he thought about his meeting with Nicola – a sheer coincidence of two people seeing each other after all those years! It was a chance in a million – probably more likely in a billion. He reached over and took Wendy's hand and held it to his lips before kissing it gently, then said, 'Have I told you lately that I love you?'

'I guess you have, but it could have been as long ago as last night!'

They returned to the train at Kyle, where there were, as always after a coach excursion, two or three stewards standing by the coaches of the *Royal Scotsman* with silver salvers in their hands, filled with whatever drinks they'd decided to serve on that particular day. It provided the passengers with a lovely 'welcome back on board' and they looked forward to it. Sometimes the glasses would be filled with champagne, a rum cocktail, a bloody Mary, a Pimms or, if it was an exceptionally cold and wet day, it would be hot chocolate with a tot added to it!

It was already Thursday and their last full day on board. Tom and Wendy couldn't believe how quickly their five-day holiday had gone, and now the train was about to travel from Kyle to Inverness and head east to Keith. In the afternoon the train stopped again to take them on their final excursion, which was to experience life in a traditional working Highland distillery, where, much to everyone's delight, they got to sample some of the products!

After the visit, they rejoined the train and did their packing, before having an informal dinner. The train headed south to Aberdeen, and from there the *Royal Scotsman* followed the coast through Stonehaven and Montrose before reaching Arbroath. It passed Carnoustie, with its famous golf course, then on down to Dundee, where they stabled overnight.

On Friday morning, after breakfast, the train crossed the Firth of Forth by means of the Forth Railway Bridge, arriving back at Edinburgh Waverley station around midmorning. The organization for disembarking the passengers was incredible! The luggage, which had been collected from the cabins the night before, appeared in the taxi which had been ordered for the various destinations by everyone. The train manager had faxed through from the train to order the taxis and then the stewards had taken the suitcases off the train and placed them in the various cabs. It all happened with no waiting around and apparently no hitches.

'I'm most impressed,' exclaimed Tom as they stood and watched 'operation suitcase'. He and Wendy said their goodbyes to the different stewards and the train's manager, Ian McKee. Wendy gave a big hug to their courier, Sandra, and thanked her for looking after them so well.

'I'm really sad that the trip has come to an end,' Wendy said. 'But Tom and I have already decided that we'll do it again in the not too distant future – we've loved every minute of it!'

'You make sure you do that,' replied Sandra in her lovely Scottish accent. 'A lot of folk come back for a second time and enjoy it just as much – sometimes a little bit more!' Wendy loved listening to Sandra saying the word 'little' – she pronounced it 'lit-tle' and it seemed to be included in every sentence she spoke.

Saying their goodbyes to their newly acquired friends Bob and Sue proved quite hard. Already in such a short space of time, a firm friendship had been established. They had had so much fun together on their travels and Bob and Sue had tried to persuade Tom and Wendy, without success, to stay in Scotland for a further week's holiday in Edinburgh. They were combining a week's sightseeing with the train trip they'd just done, before flying back home to the States.

'We can't I'm afraid,' replied Tom. 'Wendy's due back at college next week and I've already got lots of work sorted for me. But we'll let you know when we're over in America next year and we'll definitely spend some time with you. In the meantime, if you're coming to London – you make sure that you come and stay with us in Wimbledon!'

'Right you guys – you're on!' said Bob.

48

After having been transferred from Edinburgh station by taxi to Edinburgh Airport, Tom and Wendy had a good flight to Heathrow. Once there, Tom collected his car and they drove straight home to Wimbledon.

When the unpacking had been completed and they were well and truly installed, Tom and Wendy sat down in their chairs at either side of the fireplace with a glass of champagne. Tom had left a bottle in the fridge for their arrival back home, so that they could enjoy a private birthday celebration of their own.

Tom was the first to raise his glass and said warmly, 'Happy birthday to you, my darling! Here's to you, and may your next fifty years turn out to be very happy ones!'

'Thank you, Tom. But I hope you realize that in another fifty years, I will be one hundred! Do you honestly think that I am capable of making it that far?'

'No problem,' replied Tom, and smiled. 'You've been quite capable of making me happy over the last few years, so I'm quite certain that another fifty won't phase you!'

'Well, I guess I'll have to see what I can do, won't I? In the meantime, how about pouring me another glass of bubbly. Champagne should give me a good kick-start,' said Wendy, holding out her empty glass for a refill.

Tom got up from his chair and walked over to her. 'You can put your glass down and get up to give me one of your special hugs, then I'll pour you some more champagne.' He held out both his hands to his wife and slowly pulled her up out of the chair and into his arms. Then, before kissing her, he said, 'Oh! By the way, have I told you lately that I love you?'

'Come to think of it – no, you definitely haven't mentioned it since last night,' replied Wendy, before pressing her lips against Tom's.

That night, lying in their bed wrapped in each other's arms, Tom felt more content and at peace with the world than he had ever felt before. He had now turned sixty, but he felt more like forty. This feeling of contentment had absolutely nothing to do with age, it went far deeper than that. It was more like reading the final chapter of a good novel, where all the loose ends are tied up and everything that's gone on before makes sense.

To have met up again with Nicola in the Cuillin Hills on that bleak day on the Isle of Skye had had a distinct effect on Tom's whole attitude to life. It was a feeling that he found hard to explain, even to himself. No doubt it would take a psychotherapist to analyse it, but all that Tom did know was that he felt happy and relaxed about everything, with no regrets at all.

Maybe, Tom had always secretly wanted to see Nicola again and he had at last proved to himself that he held no hidden longings for what might have been, and he certainly had no desire to see her again. Nicola had appeared to him almost as a stranger – someone whom he had known and loved in another lifetime, a long, long, time ago.

Tom held Wendy to him and in the darkness that engulfed them he listened to the steady beating of her heart, which was pressed close to his chest. He knew that as he held her, he had everything that he needed, or would ever need, right here in his arms.